Shlomo Harary

Producer & International Distributor
eBookPro Publishing
www.ebook-pro.com

The Shoemaker's Law
Shlomo Harary

Copyright © 2022 Shlomo Harary

All rights reserved; No parts of this book may be reproduced or transmitted in any form or by any means, electronic or mechanical, including photocopying, recording, taping, or by any information retrieval system, without the permission, in writing, of the author.

Translation: Slava Bart

Contact: 1shlomoh@gmail.com
ISBN 9798415467846

THE SHOEMAKER'S LAW

SHLOMO HARARY

INTRODUCTION

In memory of my parents.

In memory of my grandmother and my aunt and uncle, who perished in the Holocaust and whose graves are unknown.

As a child I heard the stories of my family's experiences in the Holocaust.

As the years passed, I continued hearing the same stories, but with additions and expansions I wanted to know, but couldn't ask about or understand as a child.

I heard about the events of the Holocaust from my parents, my uncle, my aunts and my grandmother, as well as neighbors, the parents of friends, and other people who survived and returned home.

The genocide of Bukovina's Jewry is less known, but was no less brutal than the more well-known events of the Holocaust. Romania was not conquered by the Nazis. Rather, it was an ally to the Germans, and itself initiated the purge of its Jewry. In many cases the Romanians were crueler than the Nazis themselves. Romania was not an industrial nation like Germany, but that did not stop its citizens from murdering the Jews who lived within their territories.

At first I wrote only the tales of my own family, but I realized that larger events and processes had taken place and were worth mentioning, if only briefly. So I began searching for and gathering material that seemed relevant to those years.

I am not a historian, and this book does not presume to be historical research. In my humble opinion, the events are connected. I hope a slightly broader perspective on the events will explain them, and contribute in some small way to understanding them.

It's hard to understand how even normative and educated people become killers and savages. It must teach us where racism leads.

During the writing of this book I received much encouragement from my beloved wife Dalia and my precious daughter Hila.

I also received invaluable help all throughout the writing process from my good friend of many years, Dr. Roni Shaked of the Truman Institute at the Hebrew University in Jerusalem.

I also received important assistance from other friends, to whom I am deeply grateful, including:

Yakov Yaniv, CEO of the Yitzhak Ben Zvi Institute, who was kind enough to provide important and valuable comments.

Ronit Dagan, principal of the Paula Ben Gurion School in Jerusalem, who reinforced my feeling that the book was indeed worth publishing.

Yosef (Yolko) Klein, a native of my hometown, today a resident of Haifa, who survived the Holocaust as a ten-year-old. He encouraged me to continue writing and publishing the book.

A special thanks to Ella Harel of Sial Publishing, who agreed to take on the task of editing the manuscript and turning it into a book, thanks to her talent and professionalism. I learned much from her.

CHAPTER 1

It was early August 1991, yet the ocean water was still on the chilly side. The afternoon was unusually sunny, and the sunbathers on the beach were enjoying a pleasant breeze. The waves rhythmically rolled in from the sea, washing over the soft, clean sand, punctuating the balmy silence at even intervals. Though it was the peak of summer, there weren't many people on the elite Malibu beach, and only a few of them were swimming.

Elegant villas lined the beach, their cheery façades facing the sun-spangled canvas of the Pacific. Behind them, much humbler dwellings shyly peeked out across the road. Driving along the road, you knew rich people lived on the beachfront side simply by looking at the luxury cars with their gleaming chrome sitting in the driveways.

Most folks driving north along Route 1 are either residents of the area or tourists bound for San Francisco. The coastal vistas are breathtaking. Those visiting Malibu for the first time discover that the gulf faces south, so that the sun spends the day traveling along the shore rather than rising from beyond the mountains. Up there, on the other side of those ridges, in the mystical mist of distance, Hollywood and Beverly Hills emanate a glow of their own. A silvery

Mercedes 500, making its way from LAX, turned onto Malibu Road. Behind the wheel of the Mercedes was Irving, driving slowly while telling his guests about the surroundings. Passing the Marina, Irving pointed out that it had formerly been owned by Jews, but was now run by Saudis. The previous owners had received a fair price for it and started another business elsewhere.

Malibu had been Irving's home for decades. Irving was tall, slim, and well-built, and you could tell that he played a lot of tennis. His nearly-white hair was meticulously combed, and a pair of slim half-rim eyeglasses sat firmly on a no-nonsense nose. He wore an off-white shirt, summer pants and a pair of sandals. His speech was slow and relaxed, and he had a friendly smile which he flashed often. Looking at him, nobody would ever guess this sixty-something man was a tough, exceptionally successful businessman. The Mercedes reached the spot where the road almost touched the water on one side, with tall mountains rising on the right.

"A huge landslide spilled across here last winter and buried the road," Irving was saying. "Fortunately no one got hurt, but the road was blocked for several months. By the time they moved all that dirt, the residents had suffered considerable inconvenience."

Irving had been living in Malibu since 1969. He had originally bought a wooden beach house typical of the area, but it was eventually replaced by a much more luxurious residence of a very different style. There was something Mexican about it, with a touch of captivating *je ne sais quoi*. Like the rest of the houses here, Irving's faced the ocean.

In the front seat beside Irving sat a man of about forty-five who looked younger than his age, with pale blue eyes that curiously scanned the landscape. His wife and their eight-year-old daughter were in the back seat. They were on a short visit from Israel, and this was their first time in Malibu. Although the guests were tired from their flight, the gorgeous landscape and their host's explanations aroused their curiosity and they regarded the new sights with interest, while Irving made sure to drive along the most scenic route in the area.

After about half an hour, the Mercedes reached Irving's house and disappeared into the roofed parking area. An electric door shut behind them, cutting the house off from the road. Irving's wife Gail, who had been waiting for the guests, gave them a hearty welcome. All five sat down in the spacious living room overlooking the ocean.

Irving poured chilled white wine into crystal glasses, and Coke with ice cubes for the little girl. Meanwhile the guests told Gail that because of New York air traffic, they'd had to wait inside the plane for more than an hour before takeoff. Everyone agreed that this was a common occurrence during peak season.

The guests went up to their rooms and, after refreshing showers and a short rest, changed into the clothes the maid had ironed for them in the meantime. The house was an oasis of peace and quiet. From the living room you could see the water through the wide-open sliding glass doors, which let in the pleasant chill of the breeze from the beach.

A bar stood in the corner of the living room, mostly stocked with California wines. Several tall wooden chairs of exquisite design stood by the counter. Small rugs covered the glowing parquet floor. On the other side of the bar sprawled a lounge unit with cozy armchairs. Farther back, in a spacious corner by the kitchen door, a large dinner table of dark solid wood stood surrounded by comfortable chairs. Wide and soft-carpeted stairs led to the upper floor, where the bedrooms and guest rooms were located.

The setting sun was slowly sinking into the ocean in a symphony of gold and silver and bronze, the breeze like velvet on the skin.

They went for a walk along the shore, strolling barefoot over the soft sand. Now and then a wave would wash over their feet, a friendly refreshing touch from the living, gleaming ocean. It was getting dark, and lights were coming on in the houses along the beach.

The group returned to Irving's house. The housekeeper had prepared dinner in the meanwhile. Everyone was elated, discussing plans for the coming days around the table.

Time went by quickly, and suddenly it was late evening. The wine had probably helped with that as well. The girl and the two women retired to their rooms to sleep. The two men remained seated in the living room chairs, sipping fine wine and talking against the background of murmuring waves breaking rhythmically against the shore, one after another, like the even breathing of a sleeping giant. Now and then the lights of some distant vessel twinkled, star-like, in the dark.

Irving put his glass down on the table. "Actually, I'm not tired at all," he said. "And if it's alright with you, maybe you could tell me about Aaron."

The guest took a long sip from his glass, his eyes fixed on Irving's. "Why not?" he said. "I'm not tired either. I remember I promised to tell you someday, and to be frank I'm glad you brought it up. But I should warn you, it's a rather difficult story."

"I'm a big boy now," said Irving. There was a long silence, in which nothing seemed to move but the waves of the ocean.

Minutes passed without anyone saying a word. "Where should I start?" the guest wondered aloud. "I'll start with that day in the early autumn of 1941, in Czernowitz."

Aaron and Hermina on their wedding day before the war

Aaron, Hermina and Fanny in Czernowitz before the war

CHAPTER 2

Everything was ready.

Everybody was on the horse-drawn carts, crowding together for warmth. A journey into the terrible unknown, from which no travelers returned. The place was surrounded by Romanian soldiers and gendarmes. There was no point in trying to escape. And if they tried, where could they go? The transports were routine by now. The frozen look of the people whose fear reduced them to shells of themselves made things easier for the Romanian army.

The long line began slowly to move. There was no rush. Those who did not survive the journey would only end their suffering sooner.

Aaron was sitting next to the coachman. His wife and two-month-old son were in the back, along with his mother-in-law and her daughter Rita, and his brother and sister-in-law, who was also holding a two-month-old baby, with her eldest daughter Briti crammed in between them. She was already a big girl of eight, and knew something terrible was going on, but was still too young to fully understand the meaning. Packed tightly into the cart, she was wrapped in a blanket which had gotten wet, and underneath the blanket she was wearing all the clothes she had left. Her pert little nose peeked out from the blanket, and she never took her eyes off her father who was sitting beside her. Little Briti refused to let go of her father's large and not-so-warm hand. Occasionally she would briefly glance around at what was happening, but her eyes would quickly return to her father.

The adults still couldn't process what was going on either.

So everyone sat there in the cart, forming a tight, nervous bunch against the autumn's morning chill and the relentless drizzle which had been falling since the previous night. Around one corner stood a lone soldier at the mouth of a quiet alley. Aaron pulled the reins in the soldier's direction. "You won't lose anything," he whispered in the coachman's ear.

Aaron fixed his gaze on the Romanian soldier, dressed in an old, threadbare uniform of faded green. As was customary with Romanian soldiers, he wore a double-peaked cap, one peak at the front and one at the back, and for some reason those peaks caused Aaron to recall the hat worn by the Good Soldier Švejk. You could see from a distance the sorry state of the soldier's boots, smothered in mud. His legs were wrapped to the knees with warmers of the same faded green of his uniform. His coat was soggy with rain and he stood there without a cape, his helmet hanging from his backpack; on the other shoulder was a rifle furnished with a long, thin bayonet.

The soldier gazed at the cart which had left the procession and was approaching him. *What are they up to?* he thought, looking around in case his commanding officer might suddenly show up.

The cart stopped next to him. Aaron had noticed that the soldier was alone and trying in vain to stay warm – and he decided to use the opportunity. He held out a pair of leather gloves with fur lining and addressed the soldier. "The third house from here is ours. Please let us get some blankets and we will be right back in the procession."

The soldier looked around. *Where could they go?* he thought to himself. *And if they do wander off somewhere in the night, surely they will be brought right back.*

The soldier hesitated. What was he to do? A minute's effort in letting the cart through would earn him a pair of gloves. But if the sergeant or commanding officer showed up, he would have to witness the summary execution of those in the cart and would find himself in army jail. Was it worth risking this for a few Jews whose lives weren't worth a hill of beans?

A few long moments passed. Aaron feared he had made a mistake. The soldier was positioned here so no one would get through – why would he open the barrier? He could point the rifle and shoot without hesitation. All the while Aaron kept looking straight into the soldier's eyes, while he in turn stared covetously at the gloves, peeking covertly at the cart, at the Romanian coachman, returning to look at Aaron and meeting his gaze. The soldier's hand reached for the rifle strap.

He's taking the rifle off his shoulder and will start firing on us any moment now! Aaron thought, watching the soldier's hand. A quick look around. The soldier was still alone. Neither the sergeant nor the commanding officer could be seen. Time stood still. What would happen a moment from now? Nothing would happen. Time, after all, was standing still and the cart was stuck with all its passengers beside the barrier with the lone soldier. No going back and no advancing. The barrier and the lone soldier stood between the ghetto and the rest of the city.

The soldier took hold of the strap, adjusted the rifle on his shoulder and slowly opened the barrier. The cart crossed to the other side. Aaron looked back. The Romanian soldier was already putting on the gloves and hurriedly lowering the barrier. No way back. Being caught in the alley meant certain death. But what was there to lose? Seconds and minutes crept by, stretching into unbearably long units of panic. The cart was moving, but it felt as if they were standing instead of racing away from the place.

Quickly leaving the alley, the cart passed through the desolate city streets and reached the house from which they had been evicted a few days ago. There was no one in sight. Quiet. A terrible silence had fallen over the city. Snow mixed with rain fell despondently from the leaden sludge of the sky. The air was so cold it felt like walking through ice.

The entrance to the apartment was sealed and a decree was glued to the door: "Entrance Forbidden! The property belongs to the government of Romania."

Happy with his pay, the coachman hastily made himself scarce. Once the cart disappeared around the corner, Aaron broke the seals without hesitation and got rid of the decree. He had everyone go in and breathed a sigh of relief – the house had not been looted.

"We stay here at least until tomorrow," Aaron said to the family. "They will not show up twice at the same place. Stay away from the windows and keep quiet."

Aaron looked around. Everyone sat still. They stared blankly, still paralyzed with fear. If they were caught, he would be directly responsible for their deaths, and it would probably be better than dying slowly and in pain; but meanwhile, as long as they remained alive and far from the procession, they still had a tiny chance of survival. But how? After all, Jews were being searched out everywhere. Maybe they'd make it through this night, but what would happen tomorrow? How would they acquire food? Where would they procure the money? Aaron would be immediately recognized as a Jew because of the yellow badge. Everyone was against them. Yesterday's neighbors had turned into bitter enemies. And yet perhaps someone would help — at the risk of their own lives. *What can we do? Are we to sit here and wait for our demise?*

No answers, no solutions.

CHAPTER 3

The date was etched in Aaron's memory: July 5, 1941. At eight in the morning, the Romanian army entered the city of Czernowitz.

The Romanian army entering Czernowitz, July 1941. [Photo: Yad Vashem]

Late the previous morning, a Romanian reconnaissance unit had arrived in the city, established contact with Romanian and Ukrainian civilian authorities, given orders, and, towards evening, retreated to a position outside the city.

The next morning Romanian military regiments and German

military units entered the city along its main routes: Czernowitz-Siret Road, Transylvania Street, and the Hertza-Czernowitz route. They were met with no resistance whatsoever.

The war had broken out unexpectedly. The Germans had launched an attack without prior warning on June 22, 1941. Mere days previously, Radio London had reported the concentration of very large German forces on the border with the Soviet Union. Rumors spread through the city. What would happen when the war began? The city was close to the border and the Germans could easily reach it. Fear and panic descended on the city and uncertainty dominated the streets. No one knew what tomorrow would bring.

Early in the morning of June 22, Aaron and his wife were asleep in bed. A tense silence hovered over the landscape. The first light of a new day fell upon the ancient city. Aaron, who had begun to stir but was still drowsy, lay in bed dozing like most of the citizens of Czernowitz. Wrapped in a soft cloud of near-sleep, Aaron lay listening to the silence, the silence of quietly ripening light, the sleepy heart of a city he knew and loved.

Everything changed in an instant. Thunderous explosions shook the city awake, announcing the arrival of a new day unlike any Aaron had ever known. Planes carried out sorties over the city, all but brushing the roofs of buildings, steeples and bell towers. Batteries of anti-aircraft guns positioned across the city shot at the German planes, which spat hellfire and bombs.

Russian planes appeared in the sky from the east. The German planes disappeared for a little while. Russian artillery units positioned in the city and its vicinity engaged in deafening rapid fire. German cannon shells fell in several places across the city and the surrounding landscape.

Women wailed and wept bitterly in the streets, and terrified children ran about screaming. Men were hurriedly inducted into the army and sent eastward with the retreating Soviet forces.

A plume of thick black smoke reaching for the sky in the direction of the Czernowitz airport signaled to the citizens that the airport had been bombed and was probably inoperative.

For the next few days the city streets were filled with endless rows of Soviet soldiers swiftly marching east. At night, processions of tanks filed through the streets with a loud metallic rattle. Large numbers of different units were moving east at a rapid clip.

The families of Red Army officers were evacuated first, on night trains.

Soviet Army Headquarters, in one of the buildings in the city center, was being vacated quickly, using every possible means: people were leaving in every type of thoroughly camouflaged car, train, and cart, as well as on foot. Evacuation took place mainly at night. It was feared the Germans would actually manage to surround the Russians and destroy them. Citizens who had managed to escape the Germans were not allowed to join them.

The rumors circulating among the residents of the city reached Aaron as well. There was talk of cities that had fallen to the Germans. There was the fear that Czernowitz too would quickly succumb to their ruthless onslaught. Loudspeakers placed in the city center continuously broadcast optimistic information in a vain attempt to calm the citizens.

After several days, the last of the Russian soldiers was gone, blowing up the bridges over the river Prut in an attempt to delay the eastward advance of German forces.

The citizens had been abandoned. Going out to look for food, Aaron witnessed the fires raging throughout the city. The central post office went up in flames after the explosives stored inside went off. In the hotel next door, the flames had climbed all the way to the rooftop, dancing in diabolical glee, threatening to spread to neighboring buildings. Firefighting units no longer functioned. The Russian army had confiscated all firefighting equipment, taking it east with them. Mayhem reigned in the streets. There was a steady flow of wounded citizens to the hospitals, where the staff struggled to give everyone adequate treatment. Rabble ruled the streets, plundering stores. They broke into stores and took whatever their eyes landed on – clothes, food, bedclothes, housewares – and they didn't stop until the stores were empty. In only a few days the supply of food in the city had run out. People began to panic. Food hunting began — anything and everything. Everyone was looking for food and there was no one to re-establish order.

The madness rampaging through the streets led people to seek shelter and places to hide in the far margins of the city and in neighboring villages. Village peasants surged into the city on horse-driven carts, offering transportation for the marauders and anyone else who had need of their services and the means to pay.

Suddenly, amid the mayhem, when everyone was looking desperately for food, shelter, a place to replace the apartment that had burned down, with the ongoing evacuation of the wounded, the plundering, the panic and the fear of Germans, the first cries were heard in the streets: "Death to the Jews, death to the yids!"

Aaron was horrified. His wife was in the ninth month of her pregnancy and was expected to give birth any day. And suddenly he and his wife had found themselves in the middle of a real-life nightmare. How would this end? What would become of them?

On July 2, the coordinated German-Romanian attack on the Czernowitz sector began. The purpose of the Romanian operation was to retake northern Bukovina. The region had been annexed by the USSR about a year prior. The codename of the joint German-Romanian operation was "Operation Munich." The German 11th Army attacked from the west. The third and fourth Romanian Armies attacked from the south, heading north and east after crossing the international border between Romania and the USSR. The dictator Antonescu, Prime Minister of Romania, made these entries in his diary:

1st July, 1941

08:50: Arriving at the city of Roman. A special messenger, a first lieutenant, delivers a personal letter from Adolf Hitler, Chancellor of Germany. Generals Dumitrescu and Zaharescu hand over reports on the situation. 15:00: Making decisions about the attack tomorrow, together with German General Schubert.

2nd July, 1941

06:00: A train takes us near the border. General Haufe, commander of the German expeditionary forces in Romania, is also on the train. It's raining cats and dogs. Our cars are unable to move forward. We all get into a field vehicle and eventually onto a pair of horse-driven carts. We make it to the river Prut where the forces are supposed to cross eastward. In the process, we coordinate actions with General Zukertort, commander of the German 170th Division stationed not far from here. 14:00: Meeting with the commander of the 67th infantry brigade of the Romanian army. This Colonel Commander has managed to cross the river with his units.

At 17:00 on July 5, 1941, the Third Army and Battalions 3 and 23 of the mountain climbers, under the command of Petre Dumitrescu, entered the city.

Romanian army units, under the command of junior officers and NCOs, made contact with the Romanian and Ukrainian civilian populations, who knew the city well. The army made an announcement that for three days the civilians were free to do with the Jews as they pleased, authorizing their killing.

That same day, the operation to detect Jewish houses and apartments began, starting in the neighborhoods of Monastiresti and Horcea. These suburbs, where everyone knew everyone, were inhabited by Jews, Romanians and Ukrainians. The Romanian army patrolled with local Ukrainians and Romanians, entering every house where Jews lived. Some of the Jews were able to run and hide, but most stayed. Squads shot Jews anywhere they found them — in their houses, their apartments, their hiding places, cellars, attics, and in the streets when the Jews tried to escape towards the center of the city, where they hoped to find shelter.

In addition to the massacre, a tremendous plundering of Jewish property took place, by both the soldiers and the civilian population. Everyone was free to take whatever their heart desired, or whatever was left after others had already done so, leaving only what they were unable to carry away. Though the murder and marauding had begun in the two suburbs, they soon spread to the rest of the city. For three days, shots, screams, curses and the unchecked humiliation of Jews could be heard all over the city. Thousands were killed in those three days. The precise number of dead is unknown, as no one kept records. Two giant pits were dug in the Jewish cemetery, where 250

Jews were buried in a communal grave. More graves were dug, and holes were filled with more bodies. This hell ended after three days, only to be succeeded by further trials.

In fact, the murders had begun before the Romanian army even arrived in Czernowitz.

On July 2, 1941, shortly before the attack on the Soviet Union, the Romanians invaded the Nova Sulita settlement on the very border of the country. The excuse for this was that the Jews living there had opened fire on the Romanian army. After a quick takeover, every one of the Jews in the settlement was shot.

Another border village, Ciudei, was invaded by a Romanian regiment under the command of an especially bloodthirsty officer. Between 400 and 500 Jews were massacred in a few hours. No one survived.

The day after the launch of the offensive against the USSR, a secret meeting was held at the office of the Deputy Prime Minister of Romania, Mihai Antonescu. The meeting was attended by judges and government officials from Internal Affairs who were meant to administer the conquered areas of Bukovina and Bessarabia (the Moldova of today). In a discussion concerning "ethnic and political cleansing," orders were given for ruthless treatment of the Jews. The instructions, shameless incitement to violence, prepared the ground for a pogrom. The instructions also served as the basis for banishing the Jews to Transnistria.

The town of Strojinetz, south of Czernowitz, was among the first towns captured by the Romanians. The massacre began immediately. Most Jews were shot on the spot, though some were first subjected to severe torture. Within about two days, as many as 150 victims were found. Their bodies were left in the fields, in the houses, in the churches where they hoped to find shelter, and in hiding places where they were discovered. There were Jews who were only wounded, but who died within a day or two from blood loss because no one volunteered to help them.

In the villages around the town, the pogrom raged unchecked. In one of the villages, the soldiers forced an old blind man to lead a procession of Jews towards a narrow bridge across a river. Despite the difficulty, faltering but trying his best not to disappoint his fellow villagers following him, the old Jew managed to reach the middle of the bridge, where the soldiers shot him. He fell into the water. Next they shot a woman with a baby in her arms. She fell down into the river as well, and the baby, still alive, disappeared under the water.

In one of the alleys, soldiers mobbed a Jew and shredded him with bayonets, causing him to die a horribly painful death.

In another local village, young Jewish women were raped. Several of them committed suicide soon after. The rabbi of the village was stabbed with bayonets and had his beard shaved, but managed to survive. The secretary of the community was shot after having both eyes gouged out.

These villages were home to 540 Jews. Only 80 of them remained alive after surviving a death march to Adinet.

In another village, soldiers invaded a small Jewish farm but were confronted by the mother of the household. "No one touches my cattle. Shoot me, but don't touch my cattle," she said. The soldiers shot her and her twenty-year-old daughter who had tried to protect her. A torrent of blood gushed from the mother's body, mixing with the blood of her daughter, painting everything around the dying women – the walls, the floor, the table and chairs. The soldiers took whatever they wanted. The blood on the things they carried and the bodies of the women made no impression on them. They busily moved on to the next household.

The Jews were taken out of their houses and led to a place outside the village, where an anti-tank trench had been dug. They were ordered to line up along the trench. A woman with a little girl of about five begged to spare her life and that of her daughter. The soldiers laughed. A moment before the machine guns began to fire, the mother hid the girl under her skirt. After the firing stopped, towards evening, the girl crept out from under the bodies. She was alone in Hell. She felt not much different than the river of bodies she was creeping across to the nearest blood-caked bank. She did not believe she was alive. As she climbed, her hands and feet sank into the blood-soaked earth of the bank. The trees along the trench towered darkly over her, no life in them, below them, or above. Giant, dark shoots of death, quietly swaying to the moans of those in the trench, which could be heard long after the shooting had stopped, along with the muffled crying of a baby. Only after several days did the trench fall perfectly silent. The perfection of death.

CHAPTER 4

On July 6, 1941, at 18:15, soldiers of German Einsatzgruppe 10 entered Czernowitz. This unit was part of the Einsatzgruppe units collaboratively formed in the spring of 1941 by the German Security Police and the General Security Service. Einsatzgruppe D, under Commander Ohlendorf, was stationed in the Black Eagle Hotel in the center of the city, at the corner of the Ringplatz (the central square) and Tempelgasse (the synagogue street), considered the best hotel in the city. From the day it was founded, the Black Eagle Hotel served as the meeting place of high-placed officials, bank managers, army officers and wealthy visitors.

The Germans wasted no time. They immediately contacted the Romanian gendarmerie, commanded by Major Dlushenski. The German takeover of the city had begun. Ohlendorf had clear instructions: to destroy the Jews and the Communist commissars. Over the next few days, soldiers from Einsatzgruppe 10, armed with lists prepared beforehand, went up and down the streets looking for Jews and Communists. Within two days, one hundred Jews were arrested, including many leaders of the Jewish community. Every one of them was shot. Within a few more days, the number of Jews

The Black Eagle Hotel, which served as the headquarters for Ohlendorf and his men

killed at the hands of the Germans and the Romanian army had reached five hundred individuals.

Ohlendorf's soldiers continued to scour the city. By July 8, the Germans had arrested 1,500 Jews and jailed them in the Palace of Culture. Selection began without further ado. Some of the Jews were transported to the suburbs, murdered, and buried in a mass grave. Behind the elegant façade of the Palace of Culture, selection continued apace. Surprisingly, several dozen men who had previously served as officers in the Austrian army were let go. A few dozen elderly men were also allowed to go, but were forced to jump out of the windows down into the street. The remaining men were lined up. Einsatzgruppe men walked down each line and every tenth Jew was shot. A hundred more men were shot this way. Finally the remaining Jews were told that they were free to go, and made to flee the palace. But Romanian soldiers were waiting outside, and anyone who tarried during this mass flight was shot. Hundreds more were killed this way. Another group was released later that day, after curfew had begun. Romanian soldiers patrolling the streets near the National Theater noticed them, and opened fire without warning. The survivors were arrested by the Romanians for breaching curfew. In the silence after the shooting, the dead were left lying in the street, red blood carpeting the pavement, pooling on the sidewalks, splattered on the walls of buildings. The soldiers moved on to another part of the city, to enforce curfew and kill more Jews.

Aaron remembered the first edict issued that day by the occupying forces: "All Jews leaving their homes will be put to death on the spot." The announcement had been printed in tiny letters and pasted onto the walls of buildings in several places, but in reality the news was spread by word of mouth. Not everyone had the time to see or hear the edict. In the first three days of the occupation, two thousand Jews were killed, so people told each other. The fact that many had known the victims personally only made the sense of loss and horror worse. Additionally, that same month the soldiers forced 150 young men out of their houses, took them to the edge of the city, and buried them alive.

Aaron was terrified. He was not afraid to die. But to die like this? Would this be done to his family? he thought, and his heart shrank with horror. Life had lost its normal meaning.

The Einsatzgruppe, accompanied by the gendarmes and the Romanian soldiers, continued their Jew hunt. The units moved from house to house, taking everyone: the elderly, the sick, women and infants. Thousands of Jews were held in three places in the city: the Electric Company's warehouse, the courtyard of the gendarmerie, and the municipal courtyard. There, after several hours of nerve-wracking waiting, uncertainty, fear of the unknown and ruthless beatings with rifle butts and sticks, the Jews were lined up against the walls. Two machine guns were positioned in front of them. Soldiers took their place behind the turrets and were given an order in Romanian: "Load." The soldiers cocked and pointed the guns at the Jews. The local commander addressed the horrified Jews. "In a few minutes you die," he said. These cruel theatrics repeated themselves several times, and broke their spirits. After hours of this mental torture, they were finally let go that evening, but not before they were meticulously searched and everything they carried in their pockets was confiscated.

Once again, the Jews were released after curfew had begun. Gendarme units and soldiers patrolling the streets to enforce the curfew came across the Jews and opened fire on them without warning. This time no one was detained either. That night many Jews were killed, and many more were severely wounded and died soon after.

The guest gave his drink a slight swirl, and watched the liquid lap the inside of the glass in circular motions, leaving pensive traces trickling down the tulip-shaped sides. "You know," he said, "I'm telling you about an entire community, but I am constantly thinking about the human beings who were there, the individuals. Each was a whole world we will never see again.

"One of them was the Nightingale of Czernowitz. When we were kids, Joseph Schmidt was in the synagogue's children's choir. Eventually, Joseph became a cantor and later a singer. He learned to sing in the Royal Academy of Berlin. Like all citizens of Bukovina, his native tongue was German. Radio Berlin began broadcasting his recitals, soon airing 38 operas. Thanks to Radio Berlin he became one of the most acclaimed and famous singers of that period. He performed on stages in Berlin, Vienna, Brussels, Paris, Helsinki and even New York. Joseph became a sought-after singer, known as 'the Jewish Caruso' and 'the Nightingale of Czernowitz.'

"In 1933, after the Nazis came to power, he was banned from Radio Berlin. Joseph left Germany and settled in Vienna. Despite the ban, he performed several more times in Berlin, but only for Jewish audiences. Unfortunately, 1938 saw the Germans march into Austria, and he was displaced once more. This time he went to Brussels, and in 1940 he made it to France, as yet unoccupied by the Germans, but the Vichy regime considered him a German. He was arrested and interned in a closed camp.

"In 1942 he managed to escape and successfully crossed the border into Switzerland on his own. When discovered by the authorities in Switzerland, however, he was sent to a refugee camp. He was supposed to stay there until his legal status in Switzerland was determined. Despite being a singer of world renown, and despite having a valid U.S. visa, he was denied any privileges. He had been unemployed for some time, his financial means had dwindled, and his health had deteriorated. Joseph, the universally adored and admired international superstar, found himself alone in strange Zurich, without work or a place to call home, separated from his family, starving and ill. Swiss authorities took their sweet time with his request for a work permit, and meanwhile his health continued to deteriorate. One day he collapsed in the street and was hospitalized in Zurich. Joseph received minimal treatment for his severe case of pharyngitis and was released after mere days. Although he complained of strong chest pains, he was returned to the refugee camp in Girenbad, near Zurich.

"One day Joseph was sitting in the Voldag restaurant near the camp. The owner of the restaurant recognized the famous singer and noticed his condition. He was thin and pale, with restless, melancholic eyes. His eyes said he needed shelter. Realizing he was in a frail physical and mental condition, she let him into one of the

The Choral Synagogue of Czernowitz [Photo: Yad Vashem]

rooms in her apartment, in the same building as the restaurant, and let him rest on one of the beds in a warm room. After several hours, when Joseph didn't come out of the room, the owner looked in to see how he was doing. She approached the bed and noticed that he wasn't breathing. Joseph Schmidt passed away on November 16, 1942, lonely, far from home, family and friends. A homeless refugee with no means of subsistence, with a heart condition, hungry and persecuted.

"The next day the Swiss authorities issued his work permit. He was buried in the Jewish cemetery in Friesenberg, Zurich.

"Another man who continues to haunt me…" The guest took a deep breath and went on with his story, "is the head rabbi of the city, Dr. Abraham Mark, chairman of the Mizrachi movement in Czernowitz and a member of the board of directors of the Romanian movement that represented Romanian Jewry in the Zionist Congress. Rabbi Mark combined mastery of the Torah with a broad education. He simultaneously studied at the Beth Midrash for rabbis in Vienna and at the university, where he received the degree of Doctor of Philosophy. His spouse Perele, who was of Polish origin, was likewise an educated woman, a graduate of the Faculty of Pharmacology at Czernowitz University. They had four children. The rabbi had acquired a reputation as an excellent preacher. Most of his preaching was done at the Choral Synagogue of Czernowitz, the Temple, among the most magnificent synagogues in Romania.

"Rabbi Mark was not just a person of high standing among Jews. In 1926, when the Archbishop of Czernowitz passed away, his funeral procession lingered in several places on its way to the cemetery. One stop was at the Choral Synagogue, where in the name of the city's Jewry, Rabbi Mark eulogized the late Archbishop. Great numbers of people stood listening, and only when the Rabbi finished his entire eulogy did the procession continue on its way to the Christian cemetery."

The guest stopped his flow of memories and momentarily sank into reverie. "You need to know more of the background to understanding the meaning of Rabbi Mark's arrest," he said. "The Germans demanded that the Rabbi contribute a thousand trucks to the German army, 'the community's donation.' But it was a ruse, and the Germans really wanted him to disclose where the Jewish money was in Czernowitz. After his arrest by Einsatzgruppe soldiers under the command of Captain Finger, the Rabbi was led to a building opposite the Choral Synagogue and taken to the top floor, so he could see his synagogue burning with his own eyes. The burning of synagogues had become the Germans' routine way of dealing with Jews since the Kristallnacht, when Goebbels gave his men the order to burn down the New Synagogue of Berlin.

"The Rabbi stood helpless, surrounded by smug, giggling Germans, seeing the flames leaping high above trees swaying in a storm stirred by a great fire, above the rooftops where demonic shadows leapt across, heat blasting his face, and he watched the synagogue, its magnificent Moorish dome, the vaulting arches and fascinating volutes of the façade, and the internal architectural scrollwork of the building, the Torah scrolls in their Holy Ark, going up in flames. He thought of the sixty Torah books, their Aramaic script consumed by flames, and felt reality slipping away. The Rabbi was rendered helpless and about to burst into tears. He felt feeble and about to collapse, but he held himself together, to deprive his captors of another reason to feel smug, and his face remained impassive. Where sacred music in stone had once stood, a charred carcass smoldered.

"All this failed to satisfy the Germans. Rabbi Mark was thrown into an improvised cell, formerly an elevator cabin, where he was ruthlessly tortured for two days, then led to a hill on the banks of the river Prut, where he was shot along with several hundred other Jews brought there from confinement in the Palace of Culture. Thousands of Jews were killed during those days of Hell.

"Other Jews had to bury the dead in mass graves, without identifying the bodies. Without names. Without papers. The Jewish community published the number of victims: 5,000 men, women, and children."

CHAPTER 5

"Over the years I've thought of more than just the people who died; I've often wondered about who was responsible, who pulled the strings, who initiated and who collaborated and who allowed the horror? Two key figures come to mind in this respect: Gruppenführer Ohlendorf, and Antonescu, the leader of Romania. The Germans under Otto Ohlendorf had a clear goal: the extermination of Jews.

"Otto Ohlendorf was born in 1907 in Hoheneggelsen, a village near Hanover, to a family of Protestant farmers. At 18, he joined the Nazi party and founded the first SS group at his place of residence. He studied law and economics at the Universities of Göttingen and Leipzig. At the same time, he was active among the student body on behalf of the Nazi party. In 1938 the young and gifted economist obtained the rank of Sturmbannführer, and a year later was appointed head of Amt III (SD-Inland) of the Reich Security Main Office (RSHA). He kept this position until 1945, when Germany was defeated and occupied by the Alliance.

"In June 1941, Ohlendorf was appointed Commander of Einsatzgruppe D, founded by Himmler alongside other units for the purpose of annihilating the Jews in the East. The unit was appended

Ohlendorf, in the International Criminal Court at Nuremberg. Condemned to death by hanging in 1951. [Photo: US Holocaust Memorial Museum]

to the 11th Army of Germany, and began operations in Soviet territories conquered by the Army. He commanded 600 soldiers and 170 vehicles which operated across Bukovina, southern Ukraine, and the Crimean peninsula. Czernowitz was the northern border of the designated area. A year after overseeing the massacre of the Jews there, he returned to Berlin and became involved in the Office of German Economy, simultaneously with his position in the Amt III. According to a report sent by Einsatzgruppe D to Berlin, Ohlendorf was responsible for the murder of 91,728 Jews in Czernowitz, Bukovina, Ukraine and the Crimean peninsula. In the Nuremberg trials, Ohlendorf described himself as an upright citizen who opposed corruption and served his country.

The allies Hitler and Antonescu shaking hands in 1941.

"In 1941, Ion Antonescu was the all-powerful dictator of Romania: an army officer with an illustrious career, a self-appointed Marshal and self-crowned 'leader' who took his cues from Hitler. While still a young officer, he had stood out for his ruthlessness and cruelty. Because of these qualities and his red hair, he was nicknamed the 'Red Dog.' During the peasant uprisings of 1907, he commanded a military unit charged with suppressing the revolt. Leading his troops against the peasants, he did not hesitate to open live fire. The results were dire for the peasants, many of whom were wounded and killed.

"He hated and abhorred Jews, and gave expression to his attitude in a meeting on April 15, 1941: 'I will grant the rabble permission to kill Jews, and after the massacre I will send in the military to impose order.' The immediate result was the horrific massacre of Jews in the city of Iasi. On the day of the massacre, Antonescu inquired about the situation in the city and ordered the commander of the city, Colonel Lupo, to drive out all the Jews. Thousands of Jews were killed during the pogrom. On another occasion, Antonescu stated that Jews were an open wound that deprived Romania's poor of their bread. Czernowitz Jews were terrified when they heard about the massacre on the radio, and knew that danger was looming. On September 6, 1941, Antonescu wrote a letter to his deputy, Mihai Antonescu: 'We have to understand that our struggle is a struggle against the Jews, not against the Slavs. If they win, we become their slaves, it's a matter of life or death.

Marshal Antonescu
[Photo: US Holocaust Memorial Museum]

We have to win and make the world pure. The war, and especially the battle of Odessa, proves that Jews are the Devil.'

"A month later, he canceled all retirement pensions for Jews. Order 8507 on October 3, 1941, was addressed to the Central Bank of Romania, and included instructions to confiscate all money and jewelry belonging to the Jews prior to their expulsion. The order was distributed by Colonel Davidescu, Marshal Antonescu's chief of staff.

"On October 4, 1941, Antonescu issued Order 6651: to expel the Jewry of Bukovina to Transnistria within ten days. General Topor undertook the order. That same month, in a meeting with his cabinet of ministers, Antonescu announced that he had decided to expel the Jews for good, and added that the goal was to chase them as far as the eastern side of the Urals, if that was possible. By the end of this period, the Red Dog and his men were responsible for the deaths of 400,000 Jews."

"I always wondered what it was about the personalities and backgrounds of these people that brought the beast out in them," Irving said.

"Yes, you could surmise all kinds of things about their upbringing and incidents in their lives, but it's impossible to understand and accept. Life's circumstances cannot explain such acts of violence," the guest replied.

"Anti-Semitism rapidly worsened. Jews were forbidden to work. The licenses of Jewish doctors were revoked and they were banned from practicing their craft. On November 15, 1940, an edict was published which allowed Jewish doctors to treat only Jews. The next day another edict proclaimed that government offices would no longer hire Jews. Jews employed by theaters and cultural institutions were fired immediately and without any compensation, journalist organizations laid off all Jewish journalists in their ranks, and the Romanian Writers' Union purged itself of all Jewish authors. Jewish lawyers could only represent Jewish clients.

"Decrees and restrictions piled on: all religious institutions in Romania were forbidden to acquire goods from Jewish stores. 'Commissars' were installed in businesses and industries belonging to Jews. Their role was simple: to ensure the Romanian nature of these organizations and reclaim them from Jewish control. Jewish companies were banned from participating in government tenders or collaborations with government-affiliated companies.

"Step after step was undertaken to shackle Jewish lives: on October 14, 1940, the Jewish cemetery in Bucharest was closed. All marine vessels owned by Jews were confiscated. Jews were no longer drafted into the military, and those still in service were immediately discharged. Jews with Romanian passports were urgently ordered to indicate the owners' Jewish nationality. All rental services due to expire were renewed automatically, except those belonging to Jews.

"Gendarmes and police units in Czernowitz forced thousands of Jews out of their homes to work on clearing the rubble of houses damaged by bombings, and repairing the bridges over the river Prut which had been destroyed by the retreating Soviets. Jews were made to work in the cold and rain, receiving no pay or even food.

"German Army divisions were stationed on the outskirts of the city, on the banks of the river Prut. German soldiers were likewise busy abusing the Jews any way they saw fit."

CHAPTER 6

Aaron was also forced to work. He did not complain. Every evening he would return to his apartment, and early the next morning he would leave for another round of forced labor along with other Jews. He demanded that his wife Hermina stay at home. At the end of each day, he marveled that his Romanian neighbors hadn't yet reported him, and that he hadn't been ousted from the apartment. For how much longer? He couldn't say. Every moment of the day, he was thinking about how to get out of this mess. What could he do against a country waging a war of annihilation on him?

At this point, a decree was issued forbidding Jews from being out in the streets after 18:00 – the start of the curfew. Aaron made sure to observe it, and was very careful in his behavior during those hours when they were allowed outside, to shop and make urgent arrangements, because during these hours the gendarmes were prone to pounce on people, sparing neither men nor women, neither the elderly nor the sick.

At the start of August 1941, Antonescu ordered Riosanu, the governor of Czernowitz, to begin secretly organizing a city ghetto for the purpose of first gathering the Jews in one place, and then expelling them to Transnistria.

Popovici, mayor. Saved twenty thousand Czernowitz Jews. Has been granted the honorific of Righteous Among the Nations.
[Photo: Yad Vashem]

The governor urgently contacted Mayor Popovici, invited him into his office, and demanded that an area somewhere in the city be designated for the ghetto. All preparations were supposed to take place secretly, so as to take the Jews by surprise. Popovici objected to the very idea of creating a ghetto, but was told that it was a direct order from Antonescu.

The mayor had no choice but to begin preparations. First and foremost, a delegation was sent out, with Antonescu's approval, to visit several places where ghettos had already been created, to learn from German know-how. The delegation first visited Frankfurt in Germany, and Lublin, Warsaw and Krakow in Poland. The mayor, who led the delegation, was trying to drag out the business in the hopes that the government would forget about the ghetto. However, the delegation included government officials, as well as a representative of the Security Service, all of whom had been appointed by Antonescu himself. They had studied the issue thoroughly, and the German experience contributed greatly to their understanding. When the delegation returned to Czernowitz, preparations began without further ado.

Unfortunately, Governor Riosanu, who likewise disapproved of the ghetto, passed away a short time after the return of the delegation. Moreover, the mayor was accused of aiding the Jews and was quickly removed from office. General Calotescu was now personally appointed by Antonescu to create the ghetto.

The Jews of the city felt that something bad was about to happen. Rumors spread. The community was gripped by a feeling of imminent danger. People were helpless in the face of the threat, but no one knew or could predict what was coming.

On September 29, 1941, a meeting was held to discuss preparations for the ghetto. Among those present was a most important guest: Karl Pflaumer, Himmler's personal representative. Pflaumer had been sent to Romania to observe the actions undertaken by the Romanians against the Jews. His role was to advise on and expedite Jewish-related matters. He explained to those present the strategic importance of the city. Being a former part of Austria, the city's railway system was still connected to it, and thus to Germany as well. The entire senior command of the Reich would pass through the city on its way to the USSR, which was about to be conquered, and south to Romania, Bulgaria and other regions, as well as of course back to Germany. The mayor was required to demonstrate a precise map of the ghetto area, and to hand it over to the governor. Preparations had reached their peak, but remained top secret.

A tense silence descended on the city. The Jews had already heard of mass expulsions from other areas in Bukovina to regions beyond the Dniester river, and were beginning to fear they would suffer a similar fate. They didn't know when it would happen, and hoped perhaps it would not happen to them at all.

The ghetto plans, methods for realizing them, and the order to do so came from Bucharest, the capital. Antonescu's signature appeared on all the documents, including the order to create the ghetto.

In a meeting that took place on October 6, 1941, Antonescu declared his intention to expel the Jews of Bukovina to Transnistria. The concentration of Jews in the ghetto would be an intermediate stage, the purpose of which would be to help Romanians with the complex task of expulsion.

One of the very first steps was to command the central bank to make all the preparations necessary to confiscate gold, jewelry and all other valuables from the Jews, as well as to change their money into the currency enforced in the conquered territories of the USSR, the value of which was many times lower than that of Romania's.

On October 9, 1941, regiments of the Romanian gendarmerie, reinforced by army units detailed specifically for this mission, took over all points of ingress, egress and approach to the city, creating a security zone around it. The deployment of forces was efficient and swift, preventing any possibility of legally leaving or illegally escaping the city.

That same day, the representative of the gendarmerie, General Topor, arrived in Czernowitz. During an improvised meeting with Governor Calutescu, the general quickly delivered verbal orders. Calutescu notified the region's military commander of the immediate expulsion of the Jews.

For this purpose, the management of the Romanian railroad system issued two freight trains of 50 cars each.

The next day, another meeting took place in the Governor's office, including Mayor Popovici, General Topor, representative of Romanian military headquarters Colonel Gheorghe Petrescu, and head of the Governor's office Major Marinescu. Calitescu declared in no uncertain terms that all Jews were to be sent to the ghetto immediately, under direct orders from Bucharest.

Alone facing the other three, Popovici expressed his protest and opposition to the expulsion. He said that history would ascribe personal responsibility for the expulsion to the Governor. He said that the expulsion was not in line with the character of the Romanian people, who were tolerant and compassionate. He went on to argue, among other things, the inadmissibility of crimes against citizens, and protested the sadism, racism and inhuman cruelty. He also tried to enumerate the difficulties of the process of expulsion, and the consequences which would come to haunt Romania during the peace conventions at the end of the war. He went on and on in the hopes of being able to influence the situation for the better, if only just a little. In the end, he added: "Mr. Governor, in the French Revolution there were 11,000 victims. Here we are considering 50,000. How do you think you will be judged by history as compared to Robespierre?"

Eventually, the governor seemed somewhat swayed by the mayor's speech. He tried to explain that there was a direct order, and that the officers with him were there to supervise and make sure the order was carried out to the letter.

The representative of the military headquarters intervened. "Mr. Mayor, what is it that irks you so much? What are you concerned about? Will the Jidanis be writing history? We are here to help you clean up the city."

The mayor did not hesitate. He looked at the arrogant officer. "With all due respect, sir, I am quite capable of cleaning up my own city by myself. And regarding history, it will not be written by Jews because the world does not belong to them alone. History will be written by the historians of the world, and don't you worry, sir, there will be a place in it for you as well."

During this exchange, the region's military commander, General Ionescu, entered the room. He looked crestfallen, flushed so deeply he looked almost dark, with an expression of profound pain in his eyes. He addressed the governor. "We can't do this. It's extremely cruel. Try aborting or changing the task. I am sorry I had to come to Bukovina to witness such an atrocity."

Despite everything, by the end of the meeting the mayor had been forced to participate in the creation of the ghetto. He agreed to take part in the hopes that he would be able to make it easier for the community somehow, and that maybe later he might be able to somehow abort the expulsion.

Popovici and Ionescu left the governor's room together. Ionescu said that the expulsion had to be prevented. He would speak with the governor one more time later that day and would try to convince him again.

The mayor returned to his office, morbidly gloomy. The staff members did not utter a word and the rooms with their high ceilings were ghostly and catacomb-like. The tension was so great that the mayor couldn't focus on his work. He would have preferred to return home, to rest a little and come to his senses.

The next morning, heads of the Jewish community were summoned to Calutescu's office, where they were read Edict 38: by 18:00 every single Jew had to be in the ghetto. Any Jews remaining in the city after that hour would be put to death on the spot. The location of the ghetto was disclosed by army officers to the community leaders, with no explanations or excuses. All Jewish property would be confiscated and turned over to the government, including their apartments and everything in them. Each person was allowed to take only that which he or she could carry – warm clothes and food for as many days as possible. They had to put their apartment keys inside an envelope, write their address and names on it, and hand it over to the authorities at the entrance to the ghetto.

The great operation of expelling and exterminating the Jews had begun.

The Jews understood immediately that their fates were sealed. They came out into the streets almost all at the same hour. There was no time to lose; there were only a few hours until 18:00. They had to decide what to take with them and what to leave behind, and the ghetto was several kilometers away. Many didn't know where to go, and chaos ensued. Fifty thousand people came out into the streets and began to move in the same direction.

Mayor Traian Popovici, hearing the wailing and crying, stood up from his chair and approached his window to look at the stream of human beings moving in one direction. Shocked and outraged, he rushed to meet with General Ionescu. The latter informed the mayor that the governor had given him Edict 38, ordering the creation of the ghetto, the previous evening, and had given him a series of additional personal instructions. Ionescu added that the expulsion was going smoothly, without protests on the part of the Jewish community.

Aaron was marching in the throng alongside Hermina with a two-month-old baby in her arms; his brother and sister-in-law, the latter also with a two-month-old in her arms and their eight-year-old daughter Briti; and his mother-in-law Fanny and her daughter Rita.

Aaron and his brother-in-law were laden with what they had managed to salvage from the apartments, and breathed heavily under the burden which grew heavier and heavier the closer they got to the ghetto. Though it was chilly October weather, the heavy load and the marching together of a closely-huddled throng of tens of thousands of people made them sweat. Aaron looked left and right, and saw rows of gendarmes standing on either side, not allowing anyone to deviate from the course or retrace their steps, even to take a few more things from their apartments. Once out of their houses, the Jews could not go back.

The expulsion of Bukovina Jews. A procession to Transnistria.
[Photo: US Holocaust Memorial Museum / National Archives and Records Administration]

CHAPTER 7

Aaron looked around. He saw his elderly 80-year-old neighbors all but collapsing under the burden of the few possessions they carried, confused and scared, desperately trying to find their way through the throng. He saw and heard babies screaming in the cold. He saw women in advanced stages of pregnancy, trying the best they could to keep up with their families.

All patients, even those in critical condition, were expelled from the Jewish hospital. Many collapsed on the sides of the road. The cold and rain spared no one as their lives came to an end in the gutter. Meanwhile, the gendarmes brought Jewish girls into the Jewish hospital and forced them to scrub away any traces of Jewishness before it was turned into a military hospital.

Aaron couldn't ignore the Christian citizens standing on the sides of the road alongside the gendarmes. They laughed and booed the Jidani. It was an opportunity to trample the Jews into the mud.

The ghetto was located downtown, in the poorest borough of the city. Once in the ghetto, many could not find shelter and had to sleep in the open, but Aaron had managed to find a place to stay, a tiny room which they shared with another family they had never met before.

```
I N S T R U C Ț I U N I
```

Comandamentul Suprem al Armatei a hotărât strângerea întregii populații evreești din Cernăuți într'un ghetou, după care va urma evacuarea din localitate.

Ca urmare, populația evreiască este invitată a se muta în ziua de 11 Octomvrie 1941, până la orele 18 în cartierul delimitat de străzile: Piața Daciei (exclusiv), strada Eminescu, str. Petre Liciu, str. Sf. Treime, str. I.C. Brătianu, Str. Prutului până la Calea ferată după care în lungul căii ferate până la întretăierea c.f. cu str. Caliceanca, de aci o linie dreaptă până în str. Pocuției, str. Anton Silvestru până la întretăierea cu strada Elena Doamna, strada Ștefan Tomșa inclusiv cimitirul evreesc, strada Cimitirului până la strada Romană, apoi strada Romană până la strada Putnei, de aci o linie dreaptă până la calea ferată, urmează pe linia ferată până la strada Petru Rareș, strada Petru Rareș până la strada aflată între străzile Wickenhauser și str. V. Măzăreanu, apoi urmează strada Războeni strada Vorobchevici, strada Mărășești, strada Mareșal Foch, xxx tae strada Romană, xxxxMxxxxxxxxxxxxxxx, strada General Averescu, str. Sf. Niculae, str. General Mircescu, str. Turcească, o linie ce merge prin spatele liceului și a Conservatorului de pe strada General Prezan trece prin spatele cartierului Diviziei, tae strada Dr. Weiss, apoi str. Regele Ferdinand mai jos de comenduirea pieței, str. Hormuzache și Piața Daciei.

Fiecare locuitor evreu poate lua cu el:
- Haine groase, îmbrăcăminte, etc.
- Hrană pe cât mai multe zile;

În total atât cât fiecare poate duce cu el, atât pentru instalare în ghettou cât și pentru evacuare, cunoscând că nimeni nu mai poate reveni la locuința avută.

Fiecare cap de familie evreu întocmește înainte de părăsirea domiciliului actual un inventar cu toate bunurile ce lasă în locuința părăsită.
La plecare ia și cheia locuinței.
Inventarul și cheia se închid în plic pe care se scrie numele și adresa locuitorului.
Plicul se predă în ghettou, la cerere.
Bolnavii se vor evacua la spitalul israelit din ghetoou.

Evreii găsiți după ora 18 în afara ghettoului vor fi împușcați.
Vor fi deasemeni împușcați toți cei ce vor opune rezistență se vor deda la acte de violență sau desordine, vor încerca sau distruge bunurile ce le-au aparținut, vor încerca să fugă din municipiu sau vor instiga pe alții la fapte ca cele de mai sus.
Evreii domiciliați deja în ghettou sunt obligați să primească pe ceilalți ce vin.

GUVERNATORUL BUCOVINEI,
General C. Calotescu

Edict for the expulsion of Czernowitz Jews, signed by Governor Calutescu. [Photo: Yad Vashem]

Aaron had the impression that all this was nothing but a bad dream, a nightmare from which he would wake at any moment. But the ghetto had no room for dreams, not even for nightmares. He constantly strained his mind, trying to figure out how to get organized, find food, survive the coming winter. Aaron decided to take advantage of even the tiniest opportunity to free himself and his family.

General Calutescu reported to Antonescu that the ghetto had become a reality, and the expulsion to Transnistria would begin soon. The plight of the Jews went from bad to worse. A massive wooden wall was erected around the ghetto, complemented by a barb-wire fence patrolled by the gendarmes.

The rules made up for the ghetto were crystal-clear: anyone leaving the territory without permission would die. Anyone who came out not wearing a white-and-blue ribbon, or trying to disguise themselves as a non-Jew, would be shot in the head. Jews who tried getting out were reported to the authorities by the Romanian citizenry.

The Jews were isolated from the world. Thousands of people were crowded into a tiny space, regardless of their previous economic and social status. They were forbidden to work anywhere, no matter the job or position, even in businesses which had until just recently belonged to them. They were forbidden to use public transport, and forbidden to bring bread into the ghetto. After a few days, food began to run out. Jews began to sell possessions at low prices, just to be able to buy a little food. Romanian women would come by the ghetto to acquire expensive items like furs, watches, jewelry, coats and shoes, all for a mere pittance.

The ghetto area had the capacity to house around ten thousand people in very crowded conditions. With forty thousand more, there was naturally no room for all. People looked for shelter from the cold, the rain and the snow in every possible place. They crowded up to thirty people per room, in corridors, cellars, garrets, sheds or barns. Those who couldn't find a place slept in the open. There was a severe shortage of drinking water, and water in general. Within several days the ghetto was overwhelmed by the stench of sweat, urine and feces. The Jews were reduced to the level of animals.

On October 12, 1941, another meeting was convened at the governor's office to discuss the running of the ghetto until the Jews were expelled to Transnistria. The mayor insisted once again on his objections, but this time he was alone. Even General Ionescu did not say a word. But Popovici wouldn't give up, and claimed the Jews had contributed significantly to the economy and culture of the country. Czernowitz wouldn't be able to sustain itself, since most specialists in most areas, like engineering, mechanics, construction, medicine, law, and architecture, were Jews, and there was no one to replace them at the moment. The results of expulsion were obvious: the city would collapse, and they were on the brink of winter. Everybody who remained in the city would suffer greatly, and the industry now contributing to the war effort would not be able to function. This in turn would mean the weakening of the war effort. Who would take responsibility for that? Popovici asked to take this into account and leave those Jews who were specialists in the city. Their expulsion was unchristian. He asked to leave those who had made real contributions to the nation: officers who had fought, war invalids, people who had contributed greatly to economic development, doctors and professionals in all areas.

At the end of his speech, a long, heavy silence fell over the room. Finally it was broken by the governor, who agreed to leave those indicated by the mayor of Czernowitz. Their number was restricted to just 120 people. The mayor would compose the list himself and hand it over to the governor.

On October 15, 1941, a long conversation took place between General Calutescu and "the Leader", Marshal Antonescu, regarding the danger of citywide collapse once all the Jews were expelled. Antonescu listened intently and understood the situation, including the weakening of the war effort. After a short while, he agreed to delay the expulsion of twenty thousand Jews required for the war effort and for the city to sustain itself. Jews required for the city to function would remain there temporarily, until Romanian replacements were found. For this purpose, the "Romaniazation Office" was established, the purpose of which was to take over Jewish property: businesses, factories and trade organizations under Jewish ownership. A Romanian manager was appointed whose job was to learn from the Jews how to operate the businesses, and then to fire all Jews and replace them with Romanians.

In the afternoon, the mayor was urgently summoned to the governor's office. Beside the governor and himself, General Ionescu and German Consul Schellhorn were also present.

The governor spoke first: "I have consulted with the Leader regarding the heavy consequences to befall the city as the result of the expulsion. The Leader has agreed to delay the expulsion of twenty thousand Jews, professionals, specialists and important executives, to prevent the collapse of the city. You know the city and those involved in the matter, and I have no time to deal with this. Therefore you are charged with compiling the lists. I will sign whatever is handed to me. Naturally I retain the right to decide otherwise if I come across anything inappropriate. I am delaying the expulsion for four days, by the end of which you need to provide me with the finalized lists."

The German Consul apologized to the governor and explained that the treatment of Jews was the internal affair of Romania, and that he could not be involved. With that, he left the office. The mayor and General Ionescu remained in charge of the task alone. The two of them would either succeed or fail in saving twenty thousand people from death.

They realized there was no time to waste. But how were they to professionally evaluate the people? Who was still in the ghetto and who was already gone? Who could filter so many people when there were no records? Who would keep records? Where would the tasks be performed? Would it be the army or the municipality? Who would corroborate the lists? There were many questions without answers. There was little time – they had to decide where to begin. Once the two realized the immensity of the task and the measure of responsibility, they reached the logical conclusion that the people who knew the Jewish community best were the Jews themselves. Therefore they had to involve the heads of the community in compiling the lists.

Popovici decided to visit the ghetto. He entered the ghetto from the side of the Jewish hospital. In the central square he came across a group of old rabbis and the heads of the community who represented various sectors like industrialists, artisans, doctors, engineers, architects, bakers – a full spectrum of professions. They began to surround the mayor, waiting in tense silence to hear what he had to say. They did not know his intentions, and the atmosphere was fraught with tension. The mayor waited until they had all gathered around him. Without uttering a word, they waited to see what news he had brought them. It was clear he had something important to tell them – why else would he venture inside the ghetto?

Popovici studied the people in front of him. He knew most of them; after all, he considered himself the father of the city and did his best to act as such, treating everyone equally. And now he had to decide who would stay and live like a slave in the city, and who would be sent to their deaths in Transnistria. And the Jews themselves would help decide the fates of thousands.

He addressed them with simple, honest words: "The Leader has decided that twenty thousand people need to stay in the city to keep it functioning and help rebuild it. You need to help me find the twenty thousand." For several long moments there was complete silence, then suddenly the rabbis were on their knees, praying, their eyes raised to the sky. People around him were kissing his hands and the rims of his coat, thanking him for what he was doing for them. Their weeping, though soft, had a powerful effect on Traian Popovici. He was shocked and found himself unable to contain his own tears. There were moments in life, Traian realized, when tears were natural for any human being.

But there was no time to waste, and the mayor came to his senses quickly. "Be at City Hall tomorrow morning, six o'clock," he told them. "We will begin working on the lists." He handed out permits which would allow them to leave the ghetto the following morning, and make their way to City Hall. These were the first of twenty thousand such permits he would issue in the near future. These were the first Jews from the ghetto whose lives were saved, at least for the time being.

Popovici knew there would be many obstacles in the days to come. It would not be easy. Would the four days provided by the governor suffice? His head was roiling with questions. He had to begin organizing matters. Permits had to be prepared. Coordination with the army, the Romaniazation Office, and the commander of the gendarmerie was needed. Trains to Transnistria had to be stopped, and this required contacting railroad management. There was much that needed to be done by morning, but his spirit was determined and his mind was already organizing the many complex tasks into a logical order. He hurried to his office and set to work. First he notified his deputy and made him part of the solution, then he called General Ionescu and laid out his plans in detail.

The general heard him out. "Wait in your office," Ionescu said finally. "I'm on my way, need to make a few additional preparations." Long past midnight, most of the preparations were complete.

CHAPTER 8

They retired to get some rest, in order to be ready for the following morning. The news of the twenty thousand permits spread fast throughout the ghetto. It was clear that most people would be expelled, and in the next several hours they wavered between despair and hope. Some people knew they had no chance of staying and looked for places to hide, hoping no one would find them. It wasn't easy. The gendarmes conducted raids specifically to discover people in hiding. Pressure on the Jews grew every day.

Among the few who found shelter in the basement of an abandoned factory was a young woman named Rosalie Beatrice Ruth Scherzer. Ruth was a native of Czernowitz who had grown up in a liberal Jewish household. Her native tongue was Austrian German, the city being part of the Austro-Hungarian Empire at the time. During World War I, she escaped with her family to Budapest and later Vienna, the capital of the empire, after the Russian army conquered Czernowitz. After the war, she and her family returned to Czernowitz. The city now belonged to Romania, but it was their home and the family continued to live there.

She enrolled at the University of Czernowitz and studied literature and philosophy. Her parents remained loyal to the Austrian crown. This was the atmosphere young Ruth grew up in, and it was her distinguishing trait when she began to write poetry in German.

In the ghetto she met a young Jewish man who was likewise gifted and a lover of poetry. He was younger than Ruth, but was an influence on her continued desire to write. The name of this gifted young man was Paul Antschel. As a boy, Paul had grown up in the city, belonging to an orthodox, Zionist, German-speaking family.

His father was a strict Zionist who wanted his young son to speak Hebrew, but the mother insisted he learn German and later Romanian because these were the languages traditionally spoken in the region where they lived. In the end, he studied German in a prestigious private school called Meisler, and simultaneously studied Hebrew in a Jewish school. The school was called Safah Ivriah ("The Hebrew Language") and indeed the emphasis was mainly on the study of Hebrew.

Shortly after celebrating his Bar Mitzvah, Paul abandoned the study of Hebrew. He was more attracted to the German language. He continued his studies in a Christian high school and matriculated in Czernowitz in 1938. That same year, Paul traveled to France via Germany, where he underwent a shocking experience, having arrived on Kristallnacht, the Night of Broken Glass. He continued on his way to France and enrolled as a medical student, but ceased his studies after a year, returned to Czernowitz and pursued the study of literature and Latin at the city university.

When the city was conquered by the Romanians and the Germans, Paul found himself trapped in the ghetto, where he met Ruth. Both of them wrote poetry and spent time in the abandoned basement, comparing their poems. They encouraged each other's work, and Paul came to exert influence over Ruth's poetic style. Paul's parents were sent to Transnistria and never returned. His father died of typhus and his mother was murdered when she became too weak to keep working. She was no longer of any use, and for that reason was shot in the head.

Paul and Ruth both survived and left Czernowitz after the war. Paul found his place in Paris. Ruth went wandering as far as America and visited many countries, but in the end she returned to Europe. She was especially fond of Italy, yet despite this, after years of wandering, she settled in Dusseldorf, where most of her friends and acquaintances lived.

Ruth became Rose Ausländer, a lyric poet who spent time writing in English and corresponded with Marianne Moore after meeting her in New York, eventually returning to write in her native German. Rose published dozens of acclaimed books of poetry. She received numerous prizes for her writing in Germany, including Germany's most prestigious prize for prose and poetry, personally awarded to her by the President of West Germany.

She died in 1988, alone, without a family. Her manuscripts and poetry are exhibited in the prestigious Heinrich Heine Institute in Germany. A plaque commemorating her life and work can be found on the wall of the otherwise ramshackle and unremarkable house in Czernowitz where she was born and lived.

Her best poetry and the most productive period of her career came at the end of her life, while she was living in a nursing home in the Jewish community of Dusseldorf. She had spent much of her life as a wanderer in exile, owning only two suitcases of belongings at the end of her life, finding both home and hope in poetry. In the poem *Mein Reich* (My Kingdom), an allusion to the Third Reich and Hitler's autobiographical manifesto, Ausländer describes her realm: "My small room / is a giant kingdom / I don't wish to rule / but to serve." She spent her life serving humanity with her poetry.

Paul settled in Paris and married a French aristocrat. He changed his name to Paul Celan and wrote exquisite poetry in French and German. The marriage did not last, and after the divorce he continued to live and write in Paris. He maintained occasional contact with Ruth, but the distance precluded a serious relationship. He was the recipient of numerous prestigious prizes for poetry in both France and Germany.

In 1970, after several hospitalizations due to depression, he jumped off the Mirabeau bridge and drowned in the Seine. His body washed ashore a short while later, and he was buried in a cemetery near Paris.

He is now considered one of the greatest poets of the 20th century and one of the greatest in German history, often placed alongside Goethe, Hölderlin and Rilke. His most renowned work, *The Death Fugue*, is a complex and hypnotic meditation on the horror and death of the Holocaust, which he wrote in a state of overwhelming guilt for having survived while his parents had not. Each of the four sections of the poem begins with the image of the speakers, a collective "we," drinking "the black milk of dawn" – an image Celan had borrowed from a 1939 poem by Rose Ausländer, who considered it an honor. Later, she used the phrase again in her poem *In Memoriam Paul Celan*: "nourished by the son / with black milk / that kept him alive / a life drowned / in ink blood."

CHAPTER 9

Czernowitz Jews had lived in the city for generations. As early as 1870 they already constituted the majority of the city's residents, speaking Yiddish and German, and actively involved in social, cultural and economic life. Czernowitz produced a thriving community of poets, writers, scientists and thinkers born and bred in the city. Over the years, Jews were twice elected to the post of mayor. Jews felt that the city was their home. Some called it "Jerusalem upon the Prut." The city's mixture of different peoples – Jews and Germans, Romanians and Ukrainians – and their cultural symbiosis created a unique atmosphere which probably did not exist anywhere outside Czernowitz.

But all this was cruelly swept away when the city was conquered by the Germans and Romanians. The city would never attain the same heights again.

At six in the morning on October 15, 1941, the morning of Simchat Torah, numerous gendarmes entered the ghetto and surrounded the immediate area.

They erected barriers to isolate different parts of the ghetto and began forcing people out of their homes, threatening, shouting, beating people left and right. Soon everyone was outside, elderly men and women barely able to carry what remained of their belongings, women, children with backpacks that were too heavy for them, sick people who should have stayed indoors. They were all shortly on the march with no idea where they were being taken. The gendarmes divided people into groups of sixty, moved them two streets away from the ghetto, and told them to wait. Seated on top of their belongings, they waited for what was to come. In the cold and rain, with no food, water or sanitary amenities, they sat and waited. At eleven o'clock there was some movement. Swearing, the gendarmes hurriedly herded them down a few more streets and left them there to wait once again. And again, several hours later, they were led down muddy roads, humiliated, some of them bewailing their fate and weeping uncontrollably.

They reached the train station, which was guarded by gendarmes armed with bayonets. A cattle train was waiting at the platform. The gendarmes crammed as many people as possible into the train, up to 50 or 60 people per car, huddled together, their belonging pressed to their chests. The doors of the cars were shut from the outside. The air inside soon became stuffy, making it hard to breathe. The train only departed close to midnight. Thus another transport to Transnistria was carried out. Prior transports had already gone out on October 13 and 14. Two thousand Jews per train. Transnistria at that time was going through one of the most severe winters in years. Jostling in the crowded train, being carried away from their homes, the places where they grew up, where generations lived out their lives and formed vibrant communities, they did not know that the most difficult part, the cruelest and most merciless, was still ahead of them.

On October 13, Antonescu described his day in his diary thus:

Stayed indoors in the morning because of the heavy snow. At

13:45 left by car to his office in Bucharest, accompanied by his wife. At 17:30 met German General Hauffe and heard his report about developments on the front. At 18:00 met with General Gianescu, who had come back from a visit to Germany and delivered a gift, a Fieseler Storch plane accompanied by a letter from Hermann Goring in which the Reichsmarschall thanked the Romanian Air Force for its assistance on the eastern front.

At 18:10 the next day he received a report on the state of agriculture in Transnistria. He devoted half an hour to the subject.

On the October 15, at 17:00, he met General Alexianu, governor of Transnistria, and discussed with him the state of agriculture and economics in the region.

Not a word was said about the deportations, the ghettos, the pillage and murder. Not a word about the terrible suffering of the Jews who had to weather the cold, rain and snow without roofs over their heads, hungry and sick – and all of it the work of a leader who signed deportation decrees but was afraid to leave his warm house because it was snowing.

Early in the morning of October 16, the central meeting room of City Hall saw a gathering of the mayor, General Ionescu and his men, City Hall staff, and representatives of the Jewish community. There was easy access from the meeting room to the rest of City Hall, to conserve time and make work efficient. Despite this, it took two days to make the first lists, containing approximately 178 names. It was clear that much more than four days would be required to complete the job.

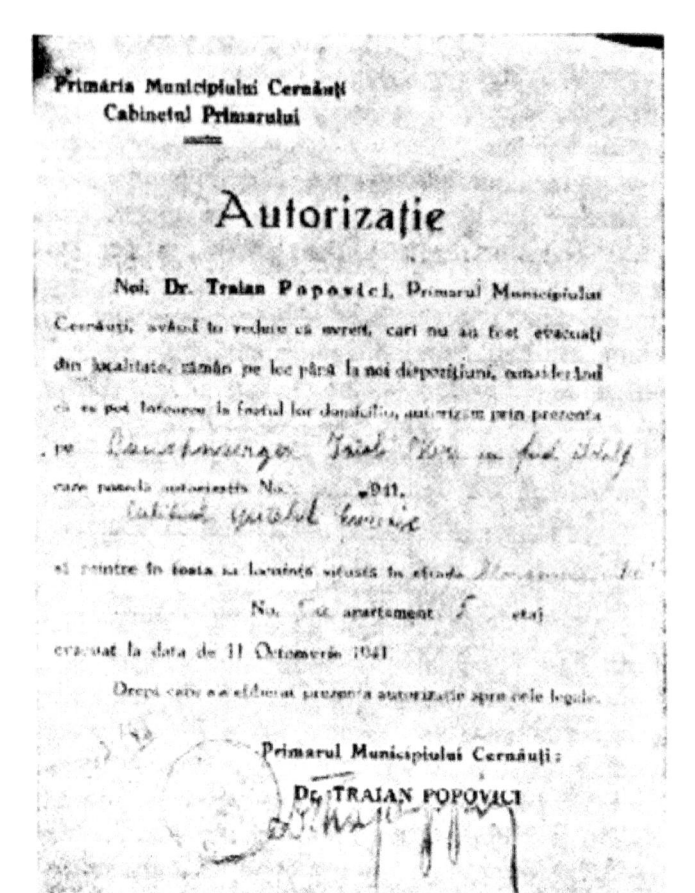

Sogenannte „Popovici-Autorisation". Durch die se Autorisationen gelang es Dr. Traian Popovici, dem Bürgermeister der Stadt Czernowitz, Tausende von Juden, vor der Deportation und dem sicheren Tode zu bewahren.

One of the permits Popovici issued [Photo: Yad Vashem]

A bitter argument developed between the mayor and the governor. The mayor pointed out the difficulties and the problems, and explained the rate at which work could be performed. In his arguments he based himself, among other things, on Antonescu's instructions not to sabotage the war effort. Popovici made an effort to convince the governor to delay further deportations from the ghetto to Transnistria until all twenty thousand permits were issued.

The mayor's efforts were successful. Further deportations were delayed time after time. Forty-eight officers of the Romanian army were present in the large City Hall meeting room, divided alphabetically into small groups, working around the clock. It took a month to complete the task. According to the mayor's estimates, under normal circumstances it would have taken several months.

But there was still more work to be done. Lists needed to be checked, adjusted to current rules, and validated by the governor, and the permits needed to be issued and distributed. The deportations to Transnistria were delayed again and again until November 15, 1941. On this date, as Popovici testified, a new and surprising order came from Antonescu: "Those Jews who have not as yet been sent to Transnistria are to remain in the city."

In July 1942, Popovici was removed from his office as mayor, after being accused of sympathy towards Jews. His position was taken by Dimitre Gallasch. One of his first decisions was to cancel the 4,500 permits issued by Popovici. The Romanians wasted no time and decided to deport all 4,500 Jews in three transports, 1,500 people per transport.

The gendarmes continued to round up Jews to carry out the deportation, but this time the task was made more difficult. The first few times the Jews were taken by surprise, but now many went into hiding. Gendarme units went out at night, accompanied by municipal clerks equipped with the precise lists of Jews. They would break into the houses belonging to the permit-holders. The Jews were given five minutes to dress and pack. They were gathered in the "Maccabi" square in the center of the city and were forced to undress completely, after which they underwent meticulous physical examinations to prevent the smuggling of valuable objects.

The gendarmes and a significant number of Romanian and Ukrainian citizens stood there, enjoying the show. The Jews stood there, humiliated and scared to death. They were deported that very night.

Two more shipments were arranged afterwards, but many of those with permits managed to hide. The gendarmes had to fulfill the deportation quotas of 1,500 per shipment. To reach those numbers, they arrested Jews who were not on the lists. Even those Jews who possessed army-issued licenses attesting to the fact that they were essential to the functioning of the city were still arrested and deported. The permits had become worthless pieces of paper.

CHAPTER 10

Aaron looked at Fritz, his brother-in-law, who was sitting in a corner beside his wife Erna. His face was expressionless, his eyes staring into empty space, and it was clear that the man was paralyzed with fear.

Fritz had not always been like that. Only two months ago, at the start of August, when Aaron's son was born, Fritz had been living in a different house nearby, twenty minutes' walk from them. But the curfew was imposed and Jews were forbidden to go out at all. Despite this, despite the great danger of being caught and paying with their lives, Fritz and his eight-year-old daughter Briti came sneaking along alleys and backyards. From doorway to dark doorway they made their way, and finally reached Aaron's apartment to be present at the bris.

Fritz had wanted to participate in the bris no matter what, and had insisted that Briti take part too. His wife had remained in the apartment with a girl born only a few days earlier. After the bris ceremony, unsurprisingly short and to the point, Fritz and Briti returned home the same way they'd come.

A few days after the bris, an apartment was vacated in the building where Aaron lived, and Fritz decided to move so the family could be close together during those hard times. They'd managed to remain together. But now he retreated into himself, sitting silently in the corner of the room, with no idea how to protect his family.

Two months after the bris, they were sent to the ghetto. Ghetto residents were deported to Transnistria, the place of exile for the Jews of Romania and Bukovina. The name was already familiar because rumors had it that Jews from the town of Kimpolung had already been deported there.

Aaron kept his thoughts to himself. They were worse off than him. There was still a small supply of food in the house, which encouraged him. They would be able to hold out for two or three days.

His mind was still teeming with thoughts. His mother, brother and sisters who lived in Kimpolung, the town of his birth, about 60 kilometers from Czernowitz, had already been sent to Transnistria. Of what had become of them, Aaron knew nothing at all. Not knowing kept him in feverish worry.

CHAPTER 11

It was long past midnight. Irving looked distressed, though he tried to maintain a calm façade. "Just a minute, I need a short break to freshen up." He got up. "Coffee?" he asked the guest. "Gladly, thank you," the guest answered. Contrary to his usual penchant for vintage white Californian wine, Irving made two cups of strong black coffee.

He took a few steps toward the sea, inhaled a lungful of salty air, and returned to his place, slumping back down. "I really needed this coffee," he said, looking into the cup's steaming black abyss after taking a sip.

They sat for a few moments in silence. Things seemed strangely unfamiliar. The darkness outside the window appeared more present than usual. Irving's oasis of the good American life seemed somehow less real than distant events and the people of a long-gone past. "I know almost nothing of the Kimpolung part of our family," Irving finally said.

The guest took a sip of the coffee, put the cup down, and sat still for a moment, gathering his thoughts. "Alright, I will tell you about the family," he said.

CHAPTER 12

Aaron's father, Rabbi Shloime Leib, lived with his family in a suburb of the town of Kimpolung. The Romanian meaning of the name is "long valley," and the town was indeed located in a long and narrow valley in the Carpathian mountains of the Bukovina region, along a railway leading into Moldova, about a hundred kilometers from the city of Iasi. A trade route passed through the town connecting Hungary and Moldova via Transylvania.

Kimpolung. The main street in 1922

About 70 kilometers north of Kimpolung stood the great city of Czernowitz, capital of Bukovina. Kimpolung is surrounded by large mountains covered in conifers. The Moldova river cuts through the length of the city, flowing through the long valley from west to east, with many smaller tributaries descending towards it from the mountainside. The town was small, about 15,000 residents in all, approximately 1,400 of them Jewish.

Before the first World War, the region had belonged to the Austro-Hungarian Empire, and even after its annexation by Romania at the end of that war, the residents continued to speak Austrian German amongst themselves. Even the Romanian peasant living next to Rabbi Shloime spoke German. However, the fact that Rabbi Shloime's household spoke Yiddish never bothered any of his Romanian neighbors.

Rabbi Shloime was a devout, observant Jew. To support his family he ran a humble grocery store in addition to a small farm owned by the family and located behind the house, on the southern side of the mountain.

The rabbi's children were born in this house, and from a young age were taught to help with the farm work and at the store. The store and the house attracted many people, Jew and gentile alike.

Rabbi Shloime would receive his many guests in the large living room of the house. The windows in this room, framed in white-painted wood, all looked out into the main street, so you could see anyone coming and going. The windows had double panes to keep the warmth in during the long, harsh winters.

A massive wooden table with wonderfully carved legs stood in the center of the room. The table was surrounded by chairs made of the same type of wood, their backs intricately carved and decorated with the image of a pair of guardian angels at the top. Three sofas stood along the walls, where guests would sit when there was no room left at the table. In the corner farthest from the windows stood a buffet, with decorative plates, glasses and cups on display. The adjacent wall supported a library laden with religious literature. The floor of the room, likewise made of wood, was always immaculately clean and polished.

When entering the room, guests always felt it had been arranged just for them. The house was known for its hospitality, but even more so for the wisdom and sage advice the rabbi was able to dispense to his guests. Peasants from throughout the region consulted him on many diverse topics, from issues concerning the growing of crops to finance to family life and marital matters. Everyone was received with hospitality that never disappointed, and was given advice which often helped.

After the difficult years of the great war, 1914-1918, life gradually regained its normal course, as befit a resort town visited every summer by people from all over Romania. In 1931 an extraordinary tourist paid a visit to the town, a Jew from New York. After disembarking from the train he immediately boarded a cab and departed straight for Rabbi Shloime's. This was no coincidence, for where else could Uncle Louis, Aaron's uncle, his mother Mindel's brother, go?

Uncle Louis and his mother, Kimpolung 1931.

Uncle Louis with Aaron, Kimpolung 1931.

Uncle Louis had come to visit his sister after years of absence. He had left his birthplace long before the great war and settled in New York, where he had established a family. The brother and sister spent that entire night comparing memories and stories of what had happened to them over the years. They both remembered an anecdote which had occurred shortly after Louis had left. He had sent them seeds which were unfamiliar to them. In a letter he sent them he had explained when to sow them and promised that the new food source would be good for them. The seeds were sown and everyone waited for the fruit to ripen.

When the fruit was picked, there was much joy. But their cooking was followed by an even greater disappointment. Everyone agreed that the taste was awful and the fruit was simply inedible. Was this what they were eating in America? they wondered. How could a country so rich live on food like that?

Letters dispatched to America described the calamity. After a while, a new and detailed letter arrived, accompanied by a new batch of seeds. The letter mainly stressed one particular thing: under no circumstances were they to eat the fruit. They had to dig into the soil, extract the potatoes, and boil and eat those.

This time everything was right. Everyone enjoyed the new dish, which soon became a staple of their menu.

During the day Aaron took care of the guest. Though he was much younger, the two soon developed a close, intimate relationship.

Aaron, tall with strong arms, glowing blue eyes and sparkling humor, was much to his uncle's liking, as he possessed similar qualities.

Once Uncle Louis even tried to convince Aaron to go with him to America, arguing that when he was settled there he would be able to bring the rest of the family.

"What could I do in America?" Aaron asked.

"So many people are living there," his uncle said, "so can you. And whatever you are doing here, you will be able to continue there."

Aaron weighed the offer carefully. "Why should I travel that far to do there what I can do here? I will stay and build my life here," he decided. His plan was to go to Czernowitz, the big city, where he was sure to succeed. Maybe in the future, after he could stand on his own two feet, he would come visit America to see what it was like.

Uncle Louis returned to New York, and about a year later, Aaron's brother Fishel was inducted into the Romanian army.

Some time after Louis's departure, everyone noticed that Rabbi Shloime was not his former self. He sank into reverie and spent much time alone, poring over sacred literature.

Nobody knew what was happening to him, and he offered no explanations but one, while in the company of friends. He looked them in the eye and said: "There are difficult times ahead of us, more difficult than those of the past war. Many people will wander the streets without knowing where they belong and what they need to do, people will lose their homes and identities."

No one understood Rabbi Shloime's words, and he himself offered no commentary.

Several years passed. The rabbi became sick and his condition deteriorated quickly. When his time came, he said: "The son who is in the army will not make it to my funeral. And you," he addressed his wife and children, "are about to go through very difficult times." Rabbi Shloime closed his eyes and gave his soul up to God.

Many people accompanied the rabbi's coffin. Most of the town's Jews came to the funeral, of course, since everyone there knew everyone else. They lived together, prayed together, celebrated together, shared each other's joys and supported each other in times of sorrow.

But there were also many there who were not Jews, the neighbors who knew Rabbi Shloime as a childhood friend and those who became acquainted with him in later years, those who had received his wise advice and those who had been guests in his house and had experienced his hospitality. Almost the entire town accompanied the coffin. Even people from far away tried to make it when they heard of his death.

After the funeral, a hard rain quickly soaked everything, but not everyone was surprised at the sudden deluge. Those who had observed the sky during the funeral had noticed dark clouds massing beyond the mountaintops and rapidly covering the sky over the town. Lightning flashed and thunder rolled over the rooftops. Large raindrops began to fall and multiplied until a cloudburst suddenly descended on the roofs of the houses, the trees, and the streets that were suddenly empty of people. Streams came flowing down from the mountains. They swelled and became a real flood, sweeping over everything in its path. The river swelled and flooded large territories. A few sheep who failed to reach safety were swept away and disappeared under the roiling surface.

From the direction of the train station came a lone soldier, soaked through, striding hurriedly. Despite the hard rain and the rushing streams he made no attempt to hide from the weather. The soldier fought his way through the raging elements with grim determination. It was hard climbing the street against the flow of the water, but he finally made it to the main street where he found many people hiding from the rain. Most of them looked at him, and when their eyes met, he understood. Fishel had not made it in time to his father's funeral.

CHAPTER 13

"Yes," the guest sighed, "That was Rabbi Shloime. Aaron's father. But I've strayed from the main narrative. Let me go back to where I left off, October 1941, when Aaron and his family escaped the ghetto."

The night had passed. Now and then the footsteps of soldiers patrolling the streets below could be heard. It rained most of the time, and raindrops drummed against the windows. Time turned sluggish, barely moving at all. Every time they heard footsteps approaching, they stopped breathing. *Are they coming for us? Surely, they will kill us all immediately. Is it better to leave the apartment and run? But where?* The babies would fall asleep and wake up crying, as babies do. They were covered in blankets that hadn't dried yet, but there was no other choice. They couldn't allow the crying to be heard. Mothers fed their babies in the dark – anything so their presence in the apartment remained undiscovered.

Towards morning, sleep overpowered them. The family curled up close together around the babies, trying to warm them in the unheated room. In the morning, when they woke up, they saw Aaron dressed and ready to leave. He looked very different, and his family couldn't understand his goal. He wore an elegant suit, a matching fine tie, shoes which were polished and shined, a wide-brimmed hat on his head and a pair of leather gloves in his hands. Impeccably shaved, Aaron stood close by the door. Everyone understood he was about to leave, but what worried and scared everyone most of all was what was missing.

They exchanged glances. Their eyes said it all.

The yellow badge was missing from Aaron's clothes. The yellow Star of David.

"Any Jew found violating this decree will be immediately shot in the head" was the precise wording of the order.

Aaron's light blue eyes expressed a deep inner calm and great self-confidence. "I'll be back in the afternoon," he said in response to his loved ones' questioning eyes. "Before curfew. Try to make it through the day without unnecessary noise." He left without waiting for a response.

Aaron walked down the familiar streets he knew so well. His strides were a little slow, but confident. Anyone outside at the time was hurrying about their business. Here and there soldiers patrolled the streets in small groups, trying to find shelter from the rain. They scrutinized people's clothing in the hopes of discovering a yellow Star of David badge.

He saw soldiers gathering in one of the alleys. It was too late to retrace his steps or change direction; the only option was to keep going at the same pace.

Several civilians were in the alley as well. Aaron did not recognize any of them. Besides the cries coming from the soldiers, everything was quiet. As he got closer, however, he heard screams which got louder. These were inhuman screams, the shrieking of wounded animals.

Aaron found himself standing opposite the soldiers along with a few other civilians. Everyone was speaking Romanian. One of the soldiers was a major. "What have these two done?" the higher-ranking officer asked the sergeant.

"They escaped the ghetto. We found them by chance," the sergeant said curtly. Aaron stood with the other civilians. His feet seemed to weigh a ton. *Is it my turn now?* he thought.

Sprawled on the road in front of him were two male Jews. There was a large amount of blood everywhere. One was still convulsing, but seemed unconscious. He lay in a great puddle of his own blood, which was still copiously jetting out of him. The other was still conscious. His body had been sprayed with bullets. One leg was crushed, his belly had been torn open and its contents had spilled onto the sidewalk. Unbelievably, he was still alive and roaring in unimaginable pain. "Kill me, kill me," he begged the soldiers, but the soldiers stood there, pleased with themselves.

Aaron felt cold sweat form on the back of his neck and roll down his spine. Suddenly he couldn't breathe. He tried to say something, but couldn't utter a word. *Is this the end*, he thought. *Has someone already identified me? I'll be next any moment now. What do I do?*

The officer turned to the sergeant. "Don't waste any more bullets. Continue with your detail." Aaron prepared for the worst. They would be all over him in a moment. He heard a short order given. The soldiers formed a line. Another short order. "Left, right, left." The soldiers marched off in another direction, leaving the alley and disappearing behind a corner.

The crowd began to disperse. Aaron knew he had to leave. With great difficulty he lifted one foot, then the other, and gradually moved away. *No one recognized me as a Jew*, he thought, putting distance between him and the victims along with the other witnesses. The wounded man's terrible screams accompanied him for a good part of the way, but eventually faded away.

Aaron kept pacing on leaden feet. The screams of the man lying in the middle of the road continued to haunt him. He gradually remembered that he had left his family in the apartment.

Is all this real or am I dreaming? he thought. *Perhaps it's a bad dream, a nightmare? What's going on around me? Things were peaceful up until very recently. The Romanians were normal people. What happened to them all of a sudden? What are all these new rules?* Aaron kept walking, immersed in thought, asking questions in vain.

For a moment he stopped short in his tracks. A thought flashed through his mind, and he kept on walking. What new rules? There weren't any new rules. The rule was that there was no rule. The only rule was staying alive.

Aaron found himself walking down Herengasse Street. Before the war, people would come here to see and to be seen. The street's Baroque décor and the pastel-painted houses always left a deep impression on those who came here. It was the sort of street you'd see in Vienna or Paris, one of the reasons the city was called "Little Vienna." It was the most elegant street in the city.

Café "Europe" was still there, and open for business. The handsome three-story building was covered with a pointed roof. Above the entrance was a pretty arch, and above it stood the sculpture of a woman in classic Greek style, watching the people coming and going. Though it was early, customers were already seated at some of the tables. Some had ordered coffee or cake, others were engaged in conversation. Further down, he reached the famous confectionery Bonbonerie, which belonged to a Romanian named Zemphiresu. It had an elaborately decorated front door, with wide, shiny doorjambs. On each side of the door were large display windows laden with goods baked on the premises. All the cakes looked fresh. A customer entered the store, no doubt to sweeten his morning. Above the door hung an elegantly-designed lamp, of the kind you'd see above other stores down the street.

Building 16 on the same street also had a handsome, decorated entrance, with a fashionable lamp above it and a sign that said "*At The Frenchwoman's*" (*Zur Franzosin*) – a store and workshop for women's headgear. Two elegant women stood by the display window, conversing in Romanian. One of them pointed at an expensive hat in the display window and explained to her friend: "I got one just like this for the amusing price of two loaves of bread, from one of the yid women in the ghetto. Popped in there a few days ago. She actually begged me to buy the hat. Told me she was hungry and the money would help her buy bread. I paid her half what she was asking."

Aaron continued on to another street, crossing the tracks for the trams, which had resumed working in the city. The tramway had already been built in 1897, half a year ahead of Vienna, the capital city of the Empire. Thus Czernowitz had demonstrated its ambitions and abilities as a thriving and modern European city.

Much had changed since then. Vienna was no longer the capital of the Empire, but part of Germany. Czernowitz had been conquered by Romania, and a year prior to that by the USSR after a period under Romanian rule post-WWI.

After a while, Aaron finally made it to the building housing the Romanian army's headquarters. The entrance was guarded by two soldiers holding bayoneted rifles and wearing helmets. They gazed curiously at the elegant civilian approaching them.

Without losing a beat, Aaron addressed the soldiers with commanding authority and a pure Romanian accent: "Tell Colonel Munteanu that a good friend is here to see him. I'm sure he'll be glad to see me."

The soldiers, of common origin, knew very well that it was better not to mess with colonels and aristocrats. Before they had time to respond, Aaron pressed a woolen scarf into each soldier's hand and said: "A humble contribution to the war effort."

The tough looks on the soldiers' faces softened somewhat, and became more friendly. "Wait here," one of them said. Aaron waited by the soldier who remained at his post, while the other went to inquire and receive orders regarding what was to be done about the unexpected guest. Minutes stretched into infinity. In his mind he could still hear the terrible screams of the wounded man in the alley. It was difficult maintaining a calm front while everything inside him was in turmoil. Who knew what awaited him there? Maybe it was a mistake after all? There was still time to change his mind, perhaps, to turn around and retrace his steps. Maybe it really would be better. But what then?

The soldier who had left came back running, his bayoneted rifle bobbing on his shoulder.

Aaron looked at him. *No other choice anymore*, he thought. *In a moment he'll stick me with his bayonet.* Aaron closed his eyes, then opened them again.

The soldier stood in front of him. "The Colonel will receive you," he said submissively. "I'll escort you to his office." Aaron remembered the soldier who had guarded the alley from which he'd emerged yesterday. *Such a difference*, he thought to himself.

After a few minutes of following the soldier down long and somewhat murky corridors, they stopped in front of a door, which the soldier flung open. The office looked more like the lair of a businessman, and only remotely resembled a military office. A massive desk made of expensive wood was complemented by an extravagant, comfortable chair behind it, positioned close to a large window overlooking the entrance and the main street outside. A Romanian flag stood by the wall with its familiar blue, red and yellow colors. Pictures and military insignia hung from the walls. The room was pleasantly warm, a fire crackling in the fireplace and fresh pieces of wood lying ready beside it.

Colonel Munteanu rose from his chair, rounded the desk, and approached Aaron. The polished wooden floor creaked slightly under his feet. The Colonel wore a green-tinted uniform tailored to his girth, meticulously ironed and sitting well on his frame. It was obviously made of fine cloth, the sort he'd worn before the war as well. He wore low, shining black shoes, and his face was perfectly shaven except for a fashionable, well-groomed mustache. Overall, he looked like a person ready to leave for an important social occasion. The ranks were apparent on his shoulders this time, but Aaron, who knew the man, knew that it was his usual way and had always been so.

The two had known each other from before the war. Their relationship had always been friendly, and the issue of Jewishness had never come up as something that could interfere with their friendship, and especially the occasional business collaboration.

Munteanu had been drafted into the army, and had been appointed the head of logistics and supply for the district. He knew, of course, that all the Jews in Aaron's area had been put in the ghetto, from which they'd be deported to Transnistria.

The two stood facing each other. The Colonel looked at Aaron, scanning his appearance from head to toe without saying a word. He was surprised, and also knew that receiving a Jew who had escaped from the ghetto could get him into unnecessary trouble.

Aaron was the first to break the silence. "You probably remember that I'm an excellent cobbler, and on my way here I noticed that your soldiers are walking around in shoes that have been worn through. It's raining, and about a month from now it will be snowing. I'm sure you could find a use for my skills at the workshop."

Munteanu considered Aaron's words as he paced back and forth across the room. His answer came after a long silence, which seemed like an eternity to Aaron. "I have no use for cobblers at the moment. I have enough of them." Aaron froze in place. What would happen now? Will he send him straight to prison? He saw the guard's bayonet before his eyes. He looked into the eyes of the officer, but encountered a cold, harsh gaze. It was not the gaze of the man he'd known in the past. Aaron thought quickly: was everything lost? He wouldn't reveal where his family was, but would it have been better to stay together? He saw again the horrors in the alley, and shuddered. He knew this could be his own fate. He had no time for doubts.

Munteanu continued. "But I could certainly use a good work manager. And because I know you and your ability to do the job, I want you here tomorrow in work clothes."

Aaron remained frozen in place, struggling to believe that it was really happening, that he had succeeded.

"You will receive a pass saying the city needs your professional skills for the war effort," Munteanu said. "There will be no arrests or deportations of Jews in the coming days."

Aaron emerged into the street with the precious pass in his pocket. Though a pass was not always worth much in a time when life itself had lost its value, at that moment the pass was the only thing that stood between Aaron's family and death.

He began to make his way back home, to his family. Though he was in a hurry, he was careful not to walk too quickly so as not to arouse suspicion. It was cold outside. He filled his lungs with fresh air and felt better. This time he chose a different route, to stay away from that cursed alley where he had witnessed Death's grisly triumph.

Aaron made it home a short while before curfew. He briefly spoke about the pass he had managed to obtain, then he went up to the second floor of the building, took the seals off the entrance to his brother-in-law Fritz's apartment, and gave him back his home. From that day on, Aaron didn't wear the yellow badge on his lapel.

After getting the pass, Aaron left early every morning to work at Romanian Army Headquarters. Although the position did not include a salary, it was worth it, of course.

About two weeks after he began working there, he appeared before Colonel Munteanu. "Here you go, the boots you ordered." Munteanu looked at the boots. They were exactly suited to his taste, and when he tried them on he immediately felt that they were remarkably comfortable. He thought to himself that these boots would be the envy of his friends, especially given the excellent quality of the leather. It was fine, flawless and shiny like a mirror.

"Where is this leather from?" the Colonel asked. He knew for certain that there was no such leather in the army warehouses.

"You can get anything in the market outside, despite the war," Aaron replied succinctly.

The Colonel realized Aaron meant the black market, and didn't ask about the price. He thought for a while and added, "My wife will soon require a pair of elegant winter shoes."

Aaron did not hesitate to reply: "Send Madame soon, so we can take her measurements."

Before long the Colonel's wife received the gift he had promised her, a pair of elegant winter shoes made of fine leather.

Two or three months later, Aaron was busy working like a veteran cobbler. He'd learned the craft studiously from one of the Jewish cobblers who worked in the same workshop, and managed to excel at it. Aaron knew that at the moment this was perhaps his only chance of not being sent to the camps.

Aaron remembered that in the beginning, when most of the young Jewish men were sent to perform forced labor in the forests around the city, he would sneak away into the dark forest shortly after work began and sleep until evening, only to rejoin the rest when it was time to return. At home he explained: "Let the others work, not me. What's the point of that labor?"

This time it was different. Though he worked for no pay but a single meager meal per day, this was his only chance at survival and he clung to it.

One day Aaron was urgently summoned to the Colonel's office. Upon entering, he immediately sensed that something bad was about to happen. Munteanu's face was frozen and his expression was strange. Aaron had no time to think what might have happened.

"As of tonight, Jews are being sent to the ghetto again, and from there to Transnistria right away," Munteanu said. "I cannot afford for the workshop to be disrupted or for the soldiers will remain without shoes. For that reason I have ordered a soldier to be stationed at the door to your apartment. I want to make sure you stay and keep working. The soldier will do whatever is necessary to guard you."

Aaron came home in the evening. There was no guard at the door. There were still fifteen minutes before curfew, and he decided to go to the nearest store to buy a few things in case the soldier never came and they were taken during the night.

There were soldiers in the street. Barely a few steps from the building entrance, he already found himself facing a soldier who was pointing his rifle at him.

"What are you doing here, Jew?" the soldier yelled. "Go to the end of the street and climb into the truck!"

Aaron gathered himself as best he could, so as not to lose his head. The soldier had caught him off guard, and it was clear that the operation the Colonel had spoken of was underway. A quick glance at the end of the street made the situation clear. There were trucks there, and Jews were being herded into them at gunpoint.

Aaron realized he had nothing to lose. He looked straight into the soldier's eyes and spoke to him with quiet authority: "I am pure Romanian. Colonel Munteanu will not be pleased with your treatment of me."

The soldier lowered his rifle and stretched out his hand. "Show me your ID," he said.

Aaron reached into his coat pocket and slowly took out his ID, handing it to the soldier. The soldier took it and began to open it. Aaron closed his eyes and waited for the shot because the ID clearly stated "Jew."

But the shot never came. The soldier shoved the document back into Aaron's hands. "Go back into your house," he said. "Don't wander around now."

Aaron turned and quickly went inside. He was pale as a ghost and his hands were shaking. For a few minutes he lay in bed until he had calmed down a little. Suddenly there was a loud knock on the door. "Open up at once!" came a loud order. *That's it,* thought Aaron, *our turn has come.*

His wife stood in the middle of the room with the baby in her arms. There was no need for words. It was the end. Aaron opened the door. In front of him stood a tall, powerfully-built soldier. "Colonel Munteanu sent me," he said. It was a different soldier. The previous one simply hadn't known how to read.

Many Jews disappeared from the city that night. They were deported to Transnistria. In the morning the curfew was lifted, but it was clear it would be simply a matter of days before the operation resumed. Army units patrolled the streets, and anyone wearing the

Yaakov in Austrian Army uniform

yellow badge was detained and humiliated.

Fanny, Aaron's mother-in-law, and her elder daughter Rita slept that night in his apartment in the center of town, on Nicolae Filipescu 7. But the next day, after the end of the curfew, Fanny decided to return with Rita to their place in the neighborhood of Rosha, a suburb of Czernowitz, where they had a small house of their own. Fanny was part of a secular family of Austrian descent, thoroughly bourgeois in their behavior, habits, and way of life. The family lived in Kimpolung and spoke German as their native language, with only enough Romanian to interact with the neighbors.

Fanny's husband Jacob was the son of the treasurer of the Jewish community in Kimpolung. In his youth, Jacob had served as an officer in the Austrian army and was in the habit of wearing his ironed uniform and starched shirt with its high collar and bowtie. He had bright eyes, and usually combed his light brown hair back. A fashionable large mustache, the tips turned upward, lent him an air of respectability and suited the two Imperial Army decorations he always wore on his chest.

Aaron respected Fanny, who was a woman of pleasant disposition, intelligence and willpower. Though she worked hard, she cultivated a neat and well-groomed appearance: meticulously dressed in a white or bright-colored blouse, ironed and starched, with a darker skirt almost reaching her ankles, low-heeled shoes, and fashionably arranged hair around her high forehead. Her eyes were intelligent and somewhat deep-set. Although she was not tall, her upright posture gave her a noble air.

He couldn't understand how an intelligent woman could make such a decision. He pleaded with her in vain. It wasn't clear why she would leave a relatively safe place and return home. Did she think she would be safer there? Once Fanny decided on something, however, nothing could stop her. Aaron tried to convince her that the house didn't matter at the moment, that it was more important to remain alive. She could build another house, buy other property. But to no avail.

"The house has to be protected," Fanny declared with a strange, inexplicable determination.

Aaron looked at her, unable to tell whether she was serious, or whether she was perhaps telling a poor joke. In vain he looked for an answer in Fanny's eyes, the eyes he knew so well. He looked over at Rita, hoping salvation might come from there, but she only said quietly, "Whatever Mother decides."

Aaron wouldn't give up. "Look, almost everyone's gone. The army spared no one. What do you mean, protect the house? How do you intend to do that? Do you think anyone will care to ask your permission? Or do you think you're capable of resisting soldiers and even overpowering them? Do it for Rita's sake, if not yours. Let the house be. I will accompany you to look at the house once things have calmed down. But not today. Try to think logically. Look, here we have a guard at our doorstep. As long as he stands there it means the danger hasn't passed yet. The moment he leaves, we can come out." Aaron kept talking in a desperate attempt to convince Fanny to stay at his place. All the while he kept looking straight into her eyes, hoping to see a change in her disposition that would signal that his persuasive efforts were successful. But it was not to be. Her gaze remained unchanged. She waited patiently for Aaron to stop talking, to run out of arguments, to lack the words to continue.

"I'm going home. Nothing will happen there," she finally said.

Without hesitating, Fanny confidently proceeded towards the door. Rita followed without saying a word. Before she opened the door, she turned around, smiled at everyone, said goodbye and went outside. There was no need for words, and perhaps it was better not to say anything at that moment. Her eyes said everything. She went out after her mother and closed the door behind her.

Aaron couldn't believe what was happening. He couldn't understand what motivated Fanny, and understood her daughter even less. Rita was a beautiful and attractive woman, with a well-toned body and smooth black hair. Her eyes, large and beautiful, gleamed with intelligence. Her posture was noble, like Fanny's. Rita had a soprano voice of remarkable purity, like that of great and famous opera singers. When Rita sang, everyone in the vicinity stopped to listen. Lacking money, Rita had been unable to study at the conservatory and had instead worked as a clerk in the Czernowitz court. She had been known to many there: judges, lawyers, police officers, and numerous civilians who required the services of the law. Everyone had appreciated and respected her. Rita had never been short on admirers, Jewish and non-Jewish alike. When the war broke out, all the non-Jewish suitors disappeared, of course, except for one. This suitor became more enthusiastic and aggressive. He was a police officer, an investigator in the ranks of the Commissar, wielding such power and authority that no one dared meddle with him. He continued to woo her for a long time afterwards, but Rita showed no reciprocity. She withstood his forceful advances and never gave in. There were those who said that because of her stubbornness, she was sent away beyond the river Bug.

Rita, Czernowitz before the war

CHAPTER 14

The soldier standing guard at the entrance glanced at the two women leaving the building. He thought to himself that in a moment the two would turn around and go back inside. But they had already disappeared around the corner.

The next day, people from the Rosha suburb said that many people had been arrested during the night, Fanny and Rita among them. They weren't even moved to the ghetto, but taken straight to the train station. To make matters worse, there were rumors that this transport was going beyond the Bug, to an area under German control, which meant that those people would be handed over to the Germans and there was little chance that any of them would survive.

Aaron did not hesitate. He immediately left for the train station. Thoughts raced through his head. Maybe there was a chance to save them? Maybe the train was still at the station and they could be taken out of the car? Disregarding his usual precaution, he walked swiftly. He knew there was little time. He began to sweat with the effort and fear. His heart pounded. As he walked, he tried to think how he would save them. How could they be smuggled out of the station? He hoped to be able to bring them to his apartment, where the soldier continued to keep guard over the residents. He was getting close to the station. He heard the sound of wheels turning and even saw the heavy smoke billowing from the steam engine. He did his best to make it in time. The steam engine released a brief, plaintive cry, and when Aaron reached the station he saw soldiers guarding every means of entrance, keeping everyone at a distance.

Worst of all, the train was already moving and he could clearly see from a distance the last train cars leaving the station, following the locomotive north in the direction of Transnistria.

The train leaving from Czernowitz took Fanny and her daughter Rita, along with other Jews, beyond the river Bug, to the labor camp Mikhailowka, where the Germans ruled.

Fanny was always hungry, even when she slept. When she couldn't fall asleep at night, her hunger would grow stronger and memories would haunt her. Her thoughts would wander back to Bukovina, to Kimpolung. There every courtyard had fruit trees, with juicy apples, wonderful pears, and plums when they were in season.

In her dreams Fanny returned to the fertile maize fields of Bukovina, flanked by fields of potatoes. She saw the farms where cows and sheep grazed, yielding milk and meat aplenty. When she woke up and returned to reality, she would shake her head from side to side, roll her eyes and think to herself: *And now what? Now we are worth less than animals.*

After a while Fanny no longer understood what was happening around her. Confusion overwhelmed her mind and she ceased to be lucid. She did not recognize the Germans as enemies. The enemy imprinted on her mind was the Russian enemy from WWI. She began to sink into memories of the past. She remembered how during the previous war she had been left alone with her small children in their house in Kimpolung. Fanny had chosen to stay in the house, while her husband retreated with the Austrian army to Vienna.

After the retreat of the Austrian forces, the town remained without government for several days, with no rule of law and no order. Everyone knew everyone and no one hurt anyone else, but they knew it was only a matter of time before the army of the Tsar, the Russian enemy, entered the town. The Russians were preceded by rumors of their cruelty, robbing and looting, and other hair-raising stories. Everyone was scared, fearing for their lives. Nevertheless, those who stayed in the town kept close to their houses and waited for what was to come.

A few days of exhausting anticipation passed, and nothing happened. Fanny and her children went to bed one evening earlier than usual, worn out by the gathering tension.

In the middle of the night Fanny suddenly woke up. It was completely dark, but there was a great commotion. From outside came the sounds of wildly galloping horses. Despite the darkness, she could see the silhouettes of soldiers atop the horses, wielding long lances. They screamed in a foreign language, bloodcurdling screams.

Fanny gathered her children around her, shaking with fear and trying to calm the terrified children, who were too afraid even to cry. Before she could address the children, they heard loud pounding on the door, and Cossacks wearing fur hats and wielding long lances broke into their house. They moved with lightning speed from room to room, checking and spearing every nook and cranny which looked to them like a hiding place, even cushions in the wardrobes. Feathers flew in all directions like snowflakes. Despite the terror that gripped her, Fanny asked the officer in charge of the commotion: "What are you looking for? You are scaring the children."

To her great surprise the officer replied in decent German with an obvious foreign accent. "We are looking for Austrian soldiers."

"There aren't any here, they all left a few days ago, you are destroying our house."

Only then did the officer look around and see the terrified children clinging to their mother like little chicks. "Don't be afraid," the officer said, "nothing will happen to you, we have children at home too." At his command the commotion in the house stopped immediately. The soldiers went outside, where the ruckus continued unabated.

Fanny and the children locked themselves in one of the rooms, not daring to move or make a sound.

They remained so until morning. The sun rose over a quiet landscape. Through a window, Fanny watched the Russian soldiers camping and resting nearby. They were busy pitching tents. A few of them had caught chickens wandering around the yard. They killed them, plucked the feathers, cleaned them using their swords, built a fire and began roasting them.

After a while, when the meat was ready and the soldiers set to eating, the door opened, and the Russian officer came in, offering Fanny half a roasted chicken. "Take food for you and the children. No point in starving when everyone around you is eating." Fanny took the food and even found the strength to force a smile and thank the officer. Only a little while ago the chicken had belonged to one of the neighbors, or perhaps it had even been hers, but it wasn't worth thinking about.

A day or two later, Fanny heard a knock on the front door, light but insistent. She opened the door. A young woman named Elena stood there. No one knew where she had come from, but it was known she was a prostitute. She had never hurt anyone, was usually very quiet and lived in one of the side alleys of the town. She had no relatives there, and most of the residents kept away from her.

"What do you want?" Fanny asked curtly.

Elena replied in a pleading tone, "The house where I lived, Russian soldiers are now stationed there and the place has become an office. I have nowhere to go. Maybe you can help me, at least for a few days."

Fanny looked at her and couldn't understand why she had come to her, of all people. If she let her in the house, what would the neighbors say? *Better not to*, she thought, *I have small children to look after.*

But in the end she took pity on the lonely young woman. *After all, we are at war and have been conquered by a foreign enemy. Who else will help her? She is a miserable creature with no relatives or friends. These are difficult times. We should try and do what we can.*

Behind the house, in the yard, stood a small shed which had served as a kitchen in the summer, and was now empty.

"You can live in the yard shed for a few days, until you find another place to stay," Fanny said.

Elena thanked her, picked up her suitcase and went to the back of the house.

Later that same day, the Russian officer came into the house along with a tall soldier wearing a clean uniform and polished boots. Wasting no time, the officer said to Fanny, "A Russian general will occupy the big room in the front of the house. You will clear your personal belongings out of there. Leave only the bed and furniture. This soldier is the General's personal servant, and will take care of all the rest. You and the children will be able to go on living in the house."

Fanny knew there was nothing she could do. Everything had happened quickly, and she was just glad they hadn't been thrown out of the house altogether.

After she removed her belongings from the room, the servant began to prepare it for his master. Though the room was already spotless, it underwent thorough cleaning. The general's clothing was arranged in the wardrobe. The boots were polished and put in a corner. The room was meticulously organized and the sheets were spread to satisfy the General's taste. The servant knew his job. He worked fast and knew exactly what to do, and where to put each thing. It was obvious the soldier knew the General and his caprices well.

The General arrived in the evening. A blond man of average height, wearing the battle uniform of the Tsar's army. He came riding on a horse, covered in dust and sweat, but overall his appearance was neat and composed, positively shining with might and mystery, as befit a member of the aristocracy.

He descended from his horse and the servant showed him the way. When he passed Fanny, who stood by the door, he lingered a moment, lowering his head slightly for a second by way of greeting before continuing on to his room. The door shut behind him. The next morning, he got up early. Clean-shaven and wearing a spotless, ironed uniform, he left the house without saying a word, lost deep in thought. He quickly climbed into the saddle and went galloping off to the front. For several days the General's room stood empty.

Over the next few days, things began to happen in Elena's shelter. She repeatedly scheduled meetings with her clients there, many of whom were soldiers from the conquering army. Revelries took place there at night, and some of her friends joined her. Drunken soldiers came and went.

Fanny tried talking to Elena. "Look, I let you stay, no more than that. I have young girls living with me, consider my circumstances."

But Elena was full of self-confidence and did not intend to give up. "You'd better be quiet, Fanny. I can change places with you. I will live in the house and you and the children can live here, but I have a good heart and will not do that. After all, you are the wife of an Austrian officer," she concluded mockingly.

Fanny realized there was no point in arguing. Elena had the

advantage. But she still tried to think of a way to resolve the issue. "It's my house, after all, and he will protect me."

Now and then the General showed up to sleep and rest in his room. The servant continued with his daily chores. He paid no attention to the proceedings behind the house. Or perhaps he knew, but did not intervene. His only concern was his master's satisfaction. The General, a silent type, was in the habit of leaving early. He ignored the presence of Fanny and her children, and was always lost in thought, always in a hurry to enter his room and always quick to leave for the front in the morning.

Fanny also feared him. Her husband was an Austrian officer, and this meant the two men were enemies.

After a particularly raucous night in Elena's shed, Fanny decided to take drastic measures. She knew she had nothing to lose. That same night Elena had also added a band of gypsy musicians who kept playing wantonly into the night, exciting her clients even more.

In the morning, as he was about to climb into the saddle, Fanny appeared before the General and all but blocked his path. "I'm sure you know what goes on at night in the shed at the back of my house," she said. "You can see I have small children. I took pity on the woman because she doesn't have anyone. That did not mean she can take over my house because of her relationship with your soldiers, and with your permission."

The General shot a quick glance at the owner of the house and said nothing, merely climbing onto the horse and riding off. The surprised servant didn't dare breathe, and even after his master was no longer in sight he continued to stand at attention. After he came to his senses, he threw himself into scrubbing the room.

Elena continued her nightly revelries. Two gypsy violinists continued to play lively melodies to the merriment of the many soldiers huddled in the shed. A few days later the General appeared again, and as was his wont he disappeared into his room, coming out earlier than usual the next morning.

Two hours later, when Fanny came outside, she saw smoke coming from the shed's chimney. *What is Elena cooking so early in the day,* she wondered. *Will she now start working during the day as well? But why such a strong fire?*

The smoke continued to rise from the chimney for the rest of the day, and only towards evening did Fanny realize it was the General's servant heating the shed, and that it wasn't about cooking. Fanny heard him argue with Elena: "The General will be back tonight, he wants to bathe and feels like taking a sauna. I have to make sure the place is ready for when he arrives."

The General indeed arrived that same day, but very late in the evening. He took a quick bath and went to bed immediately, departing very early the next morning, but the servant kept on stoking the fire in the shed because he had received very clear orders: "Any moment now." Though the General was absent for several days, his obedient servant kept the fire going in the shed day and night.

Elena had no place to receive clients for several days, because everyone knew the General had turned the place into a private sauna. And who wanted to deal with the General? After a week or so, the heat in the shed became unbearable and Elena could no longer sleep there. So she left, gathering her clothes and leaving as she had come. Fanny and the neighbors breathed a sigh of relief. The servant kept stoking the fire for a few more days, after which the General finally appeared. As usual, he appeared at dusk, went into his room, bathed and retired to sleep. In the morning he rose a little later than usual. Passing Fanny, he addressed her for the first time. "Today I am moving to another place," he said. "Thank you for the hospitality. Clearly you are a remarkable woman. Perhaps after the war I will visit to make your husband's acquaintance. I assume we will not be wearing uniforms."

Fanny barely had time to thank him before he got on his horse and galloped away. She remained standing a while longer, firmly planted in place and deep in thought about what lay in store for her. The war still raged on, and she had not had any news from her husband. But one thing pleased her – her house had protected her. After all, she had not become a refugee. She and her children were living at home.

Remarkably clear and beautiful singing came from the house, the voice of a girl, almost a young woman. It was Rita's voice. *She hasn't sung in a long while*, Fanny thought. *Not once since the Russian General moved into my house. Strange how I didn't notice.* Fanny tiptoed into the house so as not to interfere, sitting in a chair by the room where the singing was coming from. She sat there for a long while, listening without moving.

The song came from the girl's heart. There was feeling, power and rare talent in the voice, a gift from God. When Rita finished singing, a strange silence descended on the house. Everything was very quiet. Fanny looked around and couldn't understand. When she looked outside, she was surprised to see the neighbors standing quietly in the yard, waiting for the girl to resume singing.

Dear God, Fanny thought to herself. *I have never heard my daughter sing so beautifully. With such a voice and talent, she will go far. If only this war would end already!*

The war ended. Jacob returned home to his family, but he was no longer the same person. He had come back with kidney problems, suffering and in pain. In the end, he remained confined to his bed and refused medical treatment. Jacob was mentally unable to overcome the collapse of the Austrian Empire in the war. He lost faith in doctors and in any future as such, and his condition quickly worsened.

Fanny took care of her husband with endless devotion. She prepared food he loved, bathed him, changed his sheets, and always made sure the night clothes and bedding were white as snow and freshly ironed. After a year and a half, perhaps two, during one of the long evenings of caring for her husband, Fanny heard a knock at the front door. She came to the door and opened it. It was dark outside. A man stood there. "Good evening, Madame," he said without further ado. "I hope you remember me. I am very short on time. May I see your husband for a few minutes?" At first Fanny did not recognize the man, and didn't understand what he wanted with her husband. He spoke decent German with an obvious foreign accent. But by the time he had finished speaking, she had no doubts as to who it was.

"Of course," she said, "Please, come in. He is very sick, but you can see him." The man went in and followed Fanny. He stopped by Jacob's bed. The two men looked into each other's eyes without saying a word. Jacob, suffering from severe pain, was unable to carry a conversation.

Fanny looked at the guest with curiosity. He was wearing a suit that was elegant, but worn and wrinkled. He noticed she was scrutinizing him. "I am on my way to Paris. My country has no use for men like me nowadays," he said.

Before leaving the house, he said: "I am sorry, Madame, to see your husband so ill. I had hoped to meet him after the war without uniforms, but not in such circumstances. Goodbye to you, and may God help us all."

After she was left alone, Fanny thought to herself: *This cursed war. My husband lies here on his deathbed, and the Russian General, once all-powerful, has become a refugee fleeing for his life. Not so long ago, both men wore uniforms of opposing armies, mortal enemies who fought each other. Now look at them. In their present conditions and without the uniforms, they look more human. The General is a man of principle. He came to visit my husband and neither wore their uniforms. Who needs uniforms at all?* Fanny smiled pensively to herself and remained seated for a long while.

Jacob succumbed to his illness and passed away a short time later. Fanny, who remained alone with her children, decided to sell the house and move to Czernowitz. She found a place in a suburb of the city, Rosha, and used the capital she possessed to build a house. Despite the difficulties, she was determined that she and the children should have a house of their own in Czernowitz, to replace the old one. A change of place would bring a change of luck, she hoped.

Fanny had an aunt in America who had emigrated years ago and was doing well; she had married, and maintained correspondence with Fanny. The letters came across the sea at irregular intervals, which was normal for the time, at the beginning of the century. The aunt kept her up to date on events in America, what life was like there and how it was possible to get by in the new country. When the aunt heard of Jacob's passing, she tried to help as best she could. One day another letter from the aunt arrived, but unlike previous letters, this was addressed to the eldest daughter Rita.

Besides the letter itself, which was long and detailed, the envelope included two important things: a ticket for a ship to New York, where the aunt lived, and a permit from the American immigration authorities.

Rita had doubts. She was the eldest. How could she leave her mother and sisters? She hoped to avoid going to the distant country by saying she was afraid to go by ship.

Time did not stand still, and the date of departure approached, but Rita still couldn't make up her mind. Fanny did not intervene and did not impose her opinion.

The solution to the impasse came from an unexpected direction. Rita's younger sister Mildred, whom everyone called Mila, jumped at the opportunity. "I will go instead of you," she said. "I'm not afraid of sailing."

Mila sailed away. She left Czernowitz in 1924, and came back for a visit in 1932 after she was already married. Her husband remained in New York and she came with their two daughters, Sylvia and Marilyn. Marilyn was still too young to speak, but the older Sylvia, who spoke only English at first, began to chatter in Austrian German with a pronounced New York accent after a few weeks.

Fanny was happy, and went out of her way to spoil her two granddaughters.

The visit was supposed to last two months, but after a month a letter came from Mildred's husband in New York, saying that he intended to come and settle down in Czernowitz. Mildred got up and declared decisively: "I'm going home on the first ship. My clever husband thinks of doing business here. I will allow nothing of the sort. My daughters and I are staying in New York."

After two days of preparations and excitement, Mildred and her daughters returned to New York. She parted from her family with great warmth. Everyone walked her to the train station in Czernowitz. Mila promised to come again for a visit in a few years, and that she would write often in the meanwhile.

CHAPTER 15

Fanny abruptly awoke from her reveries. Heavy rain mixed with snow showered over her. Not far from her stood Rita, in threadbare clothes, moving large stones with her bare hands. She looked at her daughter's hands. They were swollen and covered in wounds as they grasped at the icy stones without gloves. *Where does my daughter find the strength*, she asked herself.

Again the memories returned to her. She remembered their house in Kimpolung. Rita was then a very small girl, still just learning to walk, wearing a long muslin dress, always trying to get back on her feet and walk, taking one small step and falling, but getting up again, not giving up. In the end help came from an unexpected source – the family dog. They had a giant Saint Bernard with long, soft fur, a good-natured dog who always guarded the children.

Rita crawled towards the dog, took hold of its fur, and pulled and pulled until she got to her feet. After she stood, she kept her hold on the fur. The giant dog did not run away. Like an experienced, veteran guide he began to move slowly, and the child moved along with him. She learned to walk while holding onto the dog's fur, and from that day she never forgot what she'd learned or her devoted canine guide.

Even after she learned to run, the dog was always near Rita. He never left her for a moment. At night he would sleep not far from the bed. Guests could roam almost anywhere they wanted in the house, but the dog never let them approach the child or the bed.

Fanny remembered the night she was driven from her house in Rosha.

Marinescu was the new head of the Office of Jewish Affairs. He was elected in the summer of 1942. Determined to deport every last Jew from Czernowitz, he had devised his own methods. He instructed his gendarmes, policemen, and soldiers, "We wait until midnight. That is the right hour to jump the yids, while they are all fast asleep. We herd them to the train station and from there straight to Transnistria. The trains will be waiting." He spared no one, not even those with special permits to remain in the city. He tore the permits to pieces right before their eyes and said: "The permit is worth nothing to me. We want money or diamonds." Not many people had the sums demanded of them, and those who did knew that they were living on borrowed time.

At midnight they heard loud knocking on the door, accompanied by the bellowing of soldiers in Romanian and the cries of the neighbors. Fanny barely had time to get out of bed before the soldiers were already in the house.

"You have five minutes to get dressed, and you can take only as much as you can carry in your arms," was their order. Anyone who dawdled got a taste of the soldiers' short tempers, as they used their rifles to strike right and left with wanton abandon.

At the neighboring house, a few soldiers were beating down the door and screaming, "Open up now or we fire!" There was no answer from inside. Finally the soldiers knocked down the door and discovered the grisly sight of four women who had committed suicide. The bodies were spread across the floor. Beside the bodies stood an old woman carrying a half-year-old baby. The soldiers went down to the street but Marinescu's voice commanded them: "What is wrong with you? Bring them outside!" The soldiers reported what they had seen, and said they couldn't throw out an old woman. "Why?" Marinescu asked. "Sir," one of the soldiers said, "I have an old mother and a baby at home. How can I?" Marinescu stared straight into the soldier's tearful eyes with contempt, and went inside himself, dragging the old woman and the baby out with his own hands, and adding them to the others who were waiting with horror for what was to come. The soldier was charged with insubordination and imprisoned for a week.

Fanny was gripped by terror. She barely had time to dress and grab a few things she came across. She didn't even remember what she had taken.

Rita stayed close by. Her eyes were scared as she shook with cold and fear. The soldiers landed their blows indiscriminately. They struck hard and painfully, so as to spur the miserable crowd more and more, until they'd all climbed into the trucks that were waiting, ready to move.

The trucks took them to the train station, where the "reception committee" awaited them. Fanny was required to pay the full year's property taxes to the municipality, but she had no money with which to pay. The clerks were considerate, and agreed to instead take the coat that was keeping her warm.

Another clerk required that she pay the electricity bill. Again she had to part with something. This time it was a bed cover she had managed to take with her. Another station, another clerk, more things to part with. By the time they reached the end of the line, Fanny and Rita remained with only the clothes on their backs.

The final station was the most difficult. The clerks refused to show understanding or flexibility. They wanted to make sure no one was hiding anything. Resorting to the threat of the soldiers' weapons, to cursing and beatings, they forced everyone to undress. A deadly silence descended on the place. Fanny and Rita stood in a long line of naked bodies. Men, women, children and the elderly were all shaking with cold and fear. No one was in a hurry. Everyone's clothes underwent a thorough search. Afterwards, their bodies were handled just as meticulously. Fanny was paralyzed with fear, with the cold, the shame and humiliation. She barely managed to dress. Her hands were freezing. Her body ached with the beatings and shook with cold.

Rita tried helping her, though her own condition was not much better.

Fanny and Rita were loaded into a reeking cattle car. It was crammed to its utmost capacity, fifty to sixty people in each car. No toilet, no water, no seats. On the car doors the soldiers wrote with white paint: "Cattle to Transnistria." Fanny and Rita managed to find a place by the wall. There was a narrow crack there that gave them access to some fresh air.

Fanny stood by the window and looked at the train station. The night was coming to its end. Early-morning gloaming light shone upon the station, the streets, and the adjacent houses.

The train began to move. Far beyond the station, in a street which led into the city, Fanny saw the figure of a man approaching at a run. He stood there by himself. Tall and well-built. For a moment she thought it was Aaron. The train was rushing north. The station quickly disappeared behind them, and with it the figure of the man. *I must be seeing things*, she thought.

Goodbye, Bukovina, she whispered in her heart. *Will I ever come back?*

The longer the ride lasted, the worse the conditions became. The train cars were impossibly cramped, there was no room to move, they hardly ate and the stench was thick, but worst of all was the lack of drinking water. The thirst was overwhelming. No point in talking about washing hands when there is no drinking water. The primary victims were the babies and the elderly. They grew increasingly feeble. So the endless ride went on. Fanny couldn't tell if she'd been in the car for a day or two, or a month.

The train went on and on at a slow pace, like there was no end to the journey. But eventually it stopped. The doors were violently thrown open by the soldiers, who welcomed the survivors with yells, eyes filled with hatred, and blows from their rifle butts and clubs. Dead bodies remained sprawled on the floors of the cars and on the station platform, having fallen out when the doors were opened.

Bukovina Jews on the Dniester riverbank waiting to cross the river to Transnistria [Photo: Yad Vashem]

After leaving the car, they were led to the only hill in the area. They spent the night on the hill in the open air, too tired, too broken, too scared to look around at the unfamiliar place to which they had been brought.

Early in the morning, they were woken up by the shouting guards. They all descended the hill and gathered at the bank of the Dniester river. Crossing the river on rafts took them several hours. After that, they found themselves in Transnistria. There they saw for the first time what was in store for them. A long line of people in rags were shuffling along, some naked and others wrapped in newspapers. Those who fell never rose again. They lost the strength to free their feet from the swampy muck and take just one more step, and gave up their spirit. Now and then a soldier would shove a body into the ravine on the side of the road with his foot.

That was the first time Fanny and Rita beheld a death march. The sight rendered both of them helpless.

No one was protecting them, no one was trying to help. Where had they come to? Could all this be a nightmare? There was no time to think. The guards thoroughly searched their bodies and luggage. What remained of the valuables was confiscated by the officers. The soldiers took whatever they wanted.

The journey continued. Transnistria swallowed Fanny and Rita. They reached Tulchyn, a region under the command of Colonel Login.

The German "Tod" company, in charge of building Road 4, also known as the SS Road, was in need of working hands, and demanded Jews for work on the other side of the Bug river, an area under German control. The Romanians obliged, and 3000 Jews deported from Czernowitz were taken beyond the Bug, Fanny and Rita among them.

The Jews were divided into several labor camps: Mikhailowka, Tarasivka, and other camps along Road 4. This road was supposed to connect Germany and the Crimean peninsula, and continue from there to the Caucasus Mountains and the oil-rich region the Germans were hoping to reach in order to seize the resources needed to power their military.

The remains of Camp Mikhailowka [Photo: Yad Vashem]

Fanny and Rita were thrown off their truck into the muck, and were directed towards a camp gate surrounded by a metal wire fence. Inside the camp, they were ordered to form lines with the other Jews. A uniformed German stood in front of them, apparently charged with running the place, and gave a speech that was short and to the point: "Listen up. There is no status here, no differences between any of you. It doesn't matter what you did before, your studies and professions, here you are all filthy Jews. You are here to work and die. Tomorrow morning you will be sent off to work. You are forbidden to speak with those passing near the fence. Anyone who tries to escape will be caught and hanged from that post."

Fanny and Rita tried to find a corner in one of the stables which had been converted into sleeping quarters for the Jewish slaves, the property of Tod, but there was no free room for them. Eventually they slumped down to the floor, exhausted and defeated. Before she fell asleep, Fanny looked in the direction of the gate and noticed the hanging post standing there, and the rope dangling in the wind. Lacking the strength to process what she was seeing, she fell asleep.

Fanny woke up suddenly, and immediately felt a terrible fear grip her. Before she came to her senses, the screams and blows dealt out by the German and Latvian soldiers woke her up. She and Rita were sent to work at the quarry where men, women and even children worked side by side. The men crushed rock with hammers, and the women and children gathered the rubble into carts which took it to the road under construction.

The inside of the stable where Fanny and Rita were kept [Photo: Yad Vashem]

Hunger haunted them, but they only received food in the evening. At the end of each day Fanny would receive a bowl of thin pea soup, and once every seven or eight days she was given three-fourths of a loaf of bread.

When they returned to the camp after their first day of work, they found a place to sleep in one of the stables. It was a little nook for the two of them in one of the corners, with no electricity, no lamp, no light of any kind, and no water. But at least it was not out in the open. This became their new home, where they returned to sleep every night.

The train which had brought Fanny and Rita to the camp contained approximately five hundred people, including the elderly woman and the baby whose mother, together with several friends, had committed suicide when the soldiers broke into their home in Czernowitz. There were also elderly people, women who had just given birth, and a few sick people who were not suitable for hard labor. All of them were declared useless. Several days later, after work, Fanny found out that this entire group had been exterminated. They had been taken behind a hill and shot. Their bodies had been thrown into a pit dug out beforehand, and covered with a thin layer of dirt.

One day the German commander read out a list of names, those meant to be transported away. Fanny and Rita were on the list. Usually this did not bode well. People transported to other places disappeared without a trace. Fanny and Rita began to cry, and begged the German to leave them in the camp, and to their surprise he agreed. Fanny went down on her knees and kissed the German's hand in gratitude. Without saying another word, he quickly paced away and left the camp.

Despite the strict prohibition on speaking to anyone who

approached the fence, a kind of barter trade gradually developed between the Jews and local farmers.

The Jews sold their clothes, like a silk shirt left in their backpack, an elegant winter coat or a warm blanket, for something to eat, a few potatoes, a handful of flour, a little corn. The camp guards saw it and knew they were trading for food, but turned a blind eye for a little money.

The local villagers were aware of what was going on. The camp was located right inside the village, in a stable which had previously served the horses of the kolkhoz. Later on the Germans built another camp in a neighboring village, inside a schoolhouse. The need to expand the camp was the result of the constant demand for more working hands.

A new transport came from Czernowitz, 745 scared and starving Jews. They were gathered in the school. The Germans ordered them to lie down on the floor next to each other, to see how many people would have room to sleep. 107 were left outside. There was no room for them. The Germans solved the problem with their usual efficiency: they shot all 107.

CHAPTER 16

Among the people who found a place for themselves in the stable were a young couple: Mitzi Loker and her husband Bernard.

Mitzi and Bernard Loker had been thrown out of their apartment, and had had to ride to Transnistria in cattle cars for two weeks until being handed over to the Germans. Thus the couple found themselves in the Mikhailowka camp. They were immediately put to work in the quarry. The women were supposed to fill carts with stones. Every woman had to complete a quota of 21 carts per day, and woe to anyone who failed to do so. People died daily from hunger and disease. The Germans would shoot the elderly, people who had no clothes left and anyone who was too weak to work, and even dogs that strayed too near. Dead bodies were thrown into pits. Bernard told one of the Germans that dog hides could be used to make mittens and other warm items of clothing. He explained that he used to run a tannery in Czernowitz, so he would know how to work with the hides.

After a few days Mitzi and her husband found themselves in one of the houses on the fringes of the village, where they were told to begin work on the hides. The Germans brought materials as instructed by Bernard, and the couple set to it. The Ukrainian owner of the house was by all appearances a collaborator. The Lokers would come to her house early each morning, accompanied by a Ukrainian guard. After they entered, the Ukrainian woman would leave to take care of other chores.

One day Mitzi noticed a pile of onions under one of the beds. She couldn't control herself, succumbed to the terrible hunger and ate one of the onions. But once she was finished, she was beset by fear. What would become of her and her husband? Was it worth the risk? What could they do? Mitzi asked herself and her husband. In the end, she decided to confess. She approached the Ukrainian woman, told her she had stolen one of the onions because she was so hungry, and apologized. Mitzi didn't know what to expect, how the woman would respond. Would she report her to the guards? But to her surprise, the Ukrainian owner turned around and left without saying a word. The couple remained in the room and continued working, tense with expectation of what was to come. How would they be punished? Would the guards show up any minute?

Days passed. Mitzi and her husband carried on with their work in the house. The time of punishment hadn't yet come, but it was clear that it would.

One day the Ukrainian woman addressed them. "Your day has come. The Germans have dug fresh pits and are about to shoot you." Their first reaction was to think that the time for punishment had finally arrived, but on second thought they decided it was their last opportunity to escape, to run that very minute.

They looked at the owner of the house. There was no need for words or explanations. She showed them the way to a neighboring village, several kilometers in the direction of the Bug river, on the border of the territories under Romanian control.

The Ukrainian woman gave them the address of a relative in the village, and said the farmer would be willing to help. Without hesitation or wasting another moment, the couple were on their way. They snuck across fields with tall vegetation so as not to stand out. When they made it to the village, they tried to find the owner's relative, but to no avail. Mitzi knocked on a few doors, while Bernard hid in the thick undergrowth. After much searching, they found a young woman who was willing to help. She was a young and very poor woman with a newborn baby, and she hid them in the attic and provided them with food despite her economic situation.

Eleven days later the woman signaled to them to come down from the attic and into the room. They did, and found themselves facing a young farmer who was waiting for them. In the evening, the farmer signaled for them to follow him. The three began to walk, and for several hours they made their way through complete darkness. Finally they stopped to rest, and the young farmer spoke for the first time. His name was Misha. He was a partisan, a Jew, whose mission was to save Jews. He would take Mitzi and Bernard to the Romanian area.

The couple couldn't believe what they were hearing, but there was no time for reverie. The short break ended very quickly. They kept on walking all night long. During the day, they hid in the shelter of tall vegetation, away from roads so as to avoid German patrols. The journey lasted four days and four nights. On the fourth night they made it to the Bug river. Misha the partisan knew the region well, and knew where the river could be crossed on foot, where the normally-deep water only reached chest height. After crossing and resting a little, they reached the Bershad ghetto. Misha smuggled them into the ghetto and retraced his steps. Mitzi and Bernard snuck past the Romanian guards and hid amidst the tens of thousands of Jews in the ghetto. If they had been seen, they would have been shot on the spot. Eleven other people managed to escape Mikhailowka, including the artist Arnold Daghani and his wife. Only those eleven survived. The rest of the 711 people interred in the camp died.

The harsh labor under unbearable conditions continued, and Fanny's strength gradually diminished. She didn't know, and probably wouldn't care to know, that with great speed and effort the easternmost Nazi headquarters was being erected nearby. She also couldn't have imagined that Hitler himself would move into it in July 1942.

The city of Vinnitsa is located at the westernmost end of the Vinnitsa-Uman SS Road. The Mikhailowka and Tarasivka labor camps were approximately midway between the two cities. Parallel to the building of the road, intense work was being undertaken about eight kilometers north of Vinnytsia, in the direction of the city of Zhytomyr, in a dense forest. The work was being conducted by the same Tod company responsible for the SS Road.

Every single day, the construction site employed nine hundred Jewish forced laborers alongside twelve hundred Russian prisoners of war. They were building wooden houses, bunkers which might serve as shelter in case of aerial attack, communication tunnels and even caves connecting the various sites.

The entire site was surrounded by two defensive circles of metal wire and gates. Observation towers were erected, mines were spread around the site, and guard duty was entrusted to special military units. When the work was finished, extensive camouflaging was used, despite the natural cover provided by the forest surrounding the camp. Once finished, the site included living quarters and offices, hospitality areas, a swimming pool, a tea house, a sauna, and even a barbershop and a cinema, interconnected by convenient pathways. The place was even furnished with a vegetable garden. Electricity unfailingly came from the power station in Vinnytsia, backed up by a set of generators. Not far away, in Kalinovka, was an airport meant to serve this important site.

On July 16, 1942, Adolf Hitler arrived at the site. The place was built on his orders, as the closest headquarters to the eastern front, and was given the name Wolfwehr. Hitler arrived there from another site in eastern Prussia and remained until October 30 of that year.

His important generals were housed next to his quarters: Jodl and Keitel, each in a separate site within the complex. From there they directed the war, and it was from there that the order to conquer Stalingrad and the oil-rich cities of the Caucasus was issued.

Hitler remained on the premises and never left the inner security circle. Unlike him, most officers of all ranks found time to explore the nearby villages, and visit Vinnytsia to attend theater performances or to fish on the banks of the Bug river, where slaves toiled – dying forced laborers, Jews and Russian prisoners – to build the SS Road.

In the adjacent Mikhailowka, Fanny and her daughter Rita were working on this same road.

Fanny looked at Rita, straining with all her strength to lift the heavy stones. She felt some relief when she noticed Rita giving her an encouraging look. Rita's spirit was strong in spite of what was happening.

How did we ever get to Mikhailowka? thought Fanny. *This time the house in Rosha did not protect us. Maybe because it was no longer the same house from Kimpolung? Maybe I misunderstood something? Maybe I tried too hard to build a house in Rosha? If only I had stayed in Kimpolung, perhaps the good old house would have protected us.*

Fanny was jolted out of her reverie when she felt the grip of the Lithuanian soldier Wisotskas, who was suddenly dragging her to the other side of a hill. She addressed him in fine Austrian German, begging for her life: "Look what a diligent worker I am. Please let me go! I am strong, I can still work." The guard ignored her crying and pleading, determined to drag her outside the work area. "Rita, my girl, please help me!" she screamed in her daughter's direction. Rita wept bitter, heart-rending tears. She knew exactly what was about to happen, but had no way to help. Nothing at all could be done. The words of the SS officer Walter Mintel, the commander of the camp, came back to haunt her: "You have come to work and to die."

From behind the hill came a single shot.

Arnold Daghani stood there with the rest of the prisoners, watching the event unfold. His face remained expressionless and he went back to work immediately, though a storm was raging inside him. He remembered and knew to tell much later that Fanny was killed on a particular day. It was Yom Kippur, September 18, 1942.

"You understand," said the guest, swirling the drink in his glass, "Hitler and Fanny were in the same area, not very far from each other. Both were natives of Austria. Hitler had come to the place to conquer the world, Fanny had been brought against her will. Both stayed in closed sites surrounded by metal wire, under the vigilant eye of the SS.

"Hitler enjoyed comfortable conditions, the bounty of his vegetable garden, and confidence in the competence of his guard, which allowed him to stroll about safely, albeit without ever venturing beyond the camp. Trapped likewise in a neighboring site, Fanny lived in slavery, starved and tortured.

"Fanny was murdered by a Hitlerite. Three years later Hitler would take his own life. He had not conquered the world. He had brought destruction to Europe, including his beloved country – Germany."

Irving stood with his back to the guest, looking out the window. Now and then the white foam of the waves flashed in the dark, lit only by moonlight.

The guest took a deep breath. "I will go back to the events in their chronological order," he said.

CHAPTER 17

The Jews of Vinnytsia were seen as a threat to Hitler, and so in the summer of 1941 the Germans deployed Einsatzgruppen C to murder ten thousand Jews in the city and the surrounding area. Einsatzgruppen C, like Einsatzgruppen D, specialized in exterminating Jews. The unit followed in the wake of the German army, and entered every conquered territory. The units had but one mission: the extermination of Jews. Besides Arnold Daghani, another man testified as to what had happened in the region – Major Rosier, a Wehrmacht officer. He sent a report to his superiors on January 3, 1942:

> At the end of July 1941, I arrived with Infantry Regiment 52 to the Zhytomyr area, where the regiment was supposed to rest. During preparations, we heard repeated salvos of rifle fire and then gunshots. The shots were coming from somewhere nearby, and I decided to find out what it was. I departed in the direction of the sounds with Oberleutnant von Basevic and Leutnant Miller Bardman. When we arrived, we had the immediate impression that something terrible was happening, and indeed, soldiers we met there told us about executions. We took shelter behind high

ground to avoid being injured. Now and then we heard the sounds of whistling, and immediately afterwards a salvo of about ten rifle shots, followed by gunshots.

When we managed to leave our shelter, we discovered a shocking sight which was difficult to bear. We were standing on the edge of a trench about 8 meters long and 4 meters wide. The earth was piled to one side of it, and its sides streamed with unending torrents of blood. The trench was filled with the bodies of people, all ages and genders, so it was difficult to estimate its depth. Members of the Einsatzgruppen in police uniforms stood a small distance from the trench, splattered in blood, under the command of one officer. Nearby there were many soldiers in bathing suits, belonging to units stationed nearby. There were also multiple civilians, women and children. Everyone was watching what was happening. I approached the trench as closely as I could manage, and there I saw a sight I cannot forgot to this day. Amid the bodies I saw an old man with a white beard, holding a cane. He was still breathing, but it was clear that he was dying. I appealed to one of the policemen to kill him and spare him further suffering. The policeman looked at me with a smile: "I've already shot him in the stomach seven times, he will surely die on his own." The bodies lay where they had fallen. There was no effort to organize the dead. It was clear to me that many had been killed with a gunshot to the back of the head.

I took part in the war against France as well as the campaign against the USSR. I have seen many difficult sights, but never such utter horrors that I could never forget.

This report by the young German officer apparently did not merit any attention.

A little while later, after a partisan attack and the elimination of the German commander of Mikhailowka, all remaining Jews were transported to the Tarasivka camp.

At the end of October an alarm was heard in the camp. A figure was seen trying to worm its way past the metal wire and escape. The fleeing prisoner almost made it – only one foot remained within the camp. One more step to the outside. From there it would be a short distance to the trees. And in the forest – freedom!

But the bullets, which came in a long salvo from the machine gun, were faster. The soldiers approached the slumped figure and saw it was a woman. She was dead. Her eyes were open and looking at the trees in the distance. There was no fear in her gaze. Rita's mouth was open as if she had just finished a song. A thin line of blood streamed from the corner of her mouth. The clamor from a flock of birds scared by the gunshots was heard in the distance. Silence fell over the place. An autumn wind rustled the cherry trees which grew in abundance all around, and their leaves softly glided to the ground.

In the end the Germans decided to liquidate the camp. The local residents who lived nearby reported that the shots began at five in the morning. The interred Jews were led to pits that had been dug out beforehand, and there they fell when shot. The first to be executed were a father and his young daughter, and the last were two elderly men in their eighties. They approached the pit holding hands and praying. The prayer was cut short by the rapid fire of an assault rifle. Mid-prayer, they fell into the pit. This marked the middle of the day, seven hours after the shots began.

CHAPTER 18

One of the groups that arrived at Mikhailowka from Czernowitz included a girl of 18 named Selma. She was accompanied by her mother Frida and her stepfather Leo. The mother had remarried after her first husband, Max, passed away when Selma was still a little girl. She was a cousin of the poet Paul Celan, who achieved fame in Paris after the war, and like him she showed a talent for writing poetry. Selma was already writing poetry at age 15, while she was still at school. Outside of school, she was active in a socialist-leaning Jewish Zionist youth movement. The movement was supposed to prepare her for going to Palestine, to begin a new life there. She loved dancing and nature, and was an active, sprightly child.

With the outbreak of the war Selma and her parents were deported beyond the Bug river. Up to that moment, the evening of her deportation, she had managed to write 57 poems. A large number of them were love poems dedicated to her friend Leiser, who was already interred in a Romanian labor camp.

Selma Meerbaum in Czernowitz prior to the war [Photo: Yad Vashem]

Selma's friend Else was at home in Czernowitz when a strange man brought her a notebook of Selma's poetry, saying that he had received the notebook mere minutes before the gendarmes took Selma and her parents away. Selma had asked to have the notebook brought to her friend so that she would in turn pass it on to her beloved Leiser. Sometime later, Leiser returned to Czernowitz and the notebook came into his possession. When he was sent to a labor camp once again, he took the notebook with him.

Selma and her parents survived for several months. They too were forced to work at the quarry which provided stones for the building of Road 4, the SS road.

Selma managed to send a letter to Else saying that she was barely surviving, that she was afraid she would break at any moment. She ended the letter with words in Hebrew: "Love you very much, Selma."

Selma contracted typhus. Usually the SS would just shoot the sick, but Selma's parents managed to conceal her condition from the officers and she miraculously escaped that fate.

Selma attracted the attention of Arnold Daghani, who wrote in his diary: "16.12.1942, Selma Meerbaum Eisinger, toward evening she took her last breath."

Arnold's wife added to the diary: "She was running a fever and began to sing. Her voice grew more and more feeble, until it was all quiet." In one of her poems Selma writes:

I want to live.
I want to laugh and lift loads, want to fight, to love
and hate, and hold the sky in my hand, and be free
and breathe and shout: I don't want to die. No! No.

Leiser survived the camps, and in 1944 he returned to Czernowitz to look for his Selma. He had managed to hold onto his beloved's notebook, and greatly hoped to reunite with her and realize their shared dream, for which they had prepared in the youth movement before the war – to build a home in Palestine. When he despaired of ever finding Selma alive, he handed the poetry notebook to another of her childhood friends for safekeeping, asking to preserve it at all costs. "I am going to Palestine, and should anything happen to me on my way there, I would like these poems to go on living," he explained.

After a short stay, Leiser departed for Bucharest and from there to the shores of the Black Sea. There he boarded the Turkish vessel *Mefküre* along with other Jewish refugees. The ship sailed off on a symbolic date, August 5, 1944, Selma's twentieth birthday. Leiser was already twenty-one.

The passengers crowded on board were full of hope. They were finally on their way to a safe place. There they would begin new lives after everything they had endured in the camps, in Transnistria, beyond the river Bug in the German camps. After the hunger, the diseases, the death marches, the beatings of the gendarmes, the looting of their properties, the endless humiliations, after they thought there was no more hope, here they were, alive, on their way to Palestine. They would be there within days. New hopes burst into full bloom. They would start new lives and dream new dreams.

In the middle of the sea, when the sailing was smooth and most of them had laid down to rest and weave new dreams, suddenly, out of nowhere and without warning, there was a loud explosion. The ship tilted from side to side, almost tossed into the air. A torpedo from the Soviet submarine SC-215 had gutted the ship. Before anyone realized what was happening, the ship rapidly disappeared beneath the waves. All the passengers, Leiser among them, drowned.

Another of Selma's friends, Renee, returned from the camps and the notebook ended up in her possession. She did not stay in town for long. Despite all she had been through, she prepared a backpack with some belongings and her friend's poetry notebook, and started on a long and arduous journey. She traveled across all of Europe from east to west, on the roofs of trains, in horse carriages, even on foot. She crossed Poland, traversed Hungary, left Austria and Germany behind. At the conclusion of her grueling journey across Europe, she arrived in France in 1948, and from there by ship to Israel.

After several years, Selma's poems found their way into print, were translated into different languages, and received great acclaim in Germany and in other countries.

Selma's book of poetry made headlines again and again for

twenty-five years. To this day Selma is considered among the best lyric poets in the German language.

Selma did not survive. Neither did her beloved. But her wonderful poems continue to tell their story, and their love lives on.

CHAPTER 19

Aaron continued to work in the army workshop, and the Colonel continued to receive fine leather boots for his friends and relatives. At first it was only the occasional pair, but demand increased with time. And why not? The Colonel was a veteran businessman who was unwilling to settle for a wartime military salary. Why not engage in a bit of commerce? The army warehouses were well-stocked. Right under their noses, thousands of pairs of army boots were sold on the black market, not always for money but for fine leather to satisfy the tastes of many officers and their civilian kin. Those who received high-quality footwear in such hard times willingly paid top dollar, which they could easily afford. The Colonel was making good money. And what did it cost? Signing the right documents to disguise and justify the use of property belonging to the Romanian army, with transactions only in cash of course.

All parties involved in the business behaved this way, while many Romanian soldiers continued wearing shoes that were worn all the way through.

Aaron also profited, like all the Romanians involved. But he made sure to take only what was necessary to make ends meet.

And in those days, it was like owning real treasure.

One evening, loud knocking shook the door of Aaron's living quarters.

He opened the door and found a Romanian soldier dressed in combat uniform, a steel helmet on his head and a rifle slung over his shoulder. Aaron had grown used to surprises, but a soldier in combat uniform? That boded ill. It was quiet outside. The soldier was alone. *He is surely here to loot*, Aaron thought, and tried to calculate his next move. But the soldier did not appear aggressive, and Aaron couldn't understand his intentions.

"What's wrong with you, Aaron? Don't you remember me?" the soldier asked. Hearing his voice, Aaron remembered with absolute clarity: it was his neighbor Constantine, from his hometown Kimpolung.

They were the same age and had lived next door to each other. They had grown up together, gone to school together and worked the fields together. Both were powerfully built and would often wrestle.

Aaron remembered that a circus had once arrived in town and the two of them had gone together to see the show. Naturally the circus featured weightlifters – strong, muscular men. After lifting their heavy weights, they would invite members of the audience to try and lift the weights themselves. Of course no one succeeded, until Constantine's turn. He had come after a day in the fields, but still approached the weights, took hold of the pole with both hands and pulled. He almost managed to raise them all the way up, but the weights slipped out of his hands at the last second and fell. The circus weightlifters admitted that this was only due to his lack of experience.

That same evening they celebrated the event, and this time Aaron displayed his prowess. The friends took a robust length of wood and a long nail, of the sort used in wooden construction work. With a single strike of his palm, Aaron drove the nail into the wood up to its head.

Now Aaron was looking at his neighbor with cautious curiosity. It seemed he had come from afar. His face expressed fatigue and his gaze was different, not as Aaron remembered. He appeared to be pressed for time. Constantine was brief: "I'm on my way to the front, I'm only here for a few minutes to see you. I may pass through the area where your mother, sisters and brothers have been deported. Do you want to tell them anything?"

There was no time for reverie. Without hesitation Aaron took a few banknotes out of his pocket and handed them to his soldier neighbor. Then he took out another bill, the last one in his pocket, and said: "And this is for you…"

Constantine took the bill and pushed it back into Aaron's shirt pocket without saying a word. Then he took a fur hat out of his bag, of the sort farmers wore in the region where they had grown up. He offered it to Aaron. "It's mine, keep it, you might need it," he said, turning around and walking away.

Normally, such a visit would be nothing out of the ordinary, but in those days it was difficult to interpret it. Aaron thought, *If the money reaches my kin, I hope it helps them. And if not, what have I lost? Paper.*

CHAPTER 20

About two days after this incident, Aaron's cousin Moses was cooped up with his wife in their Czernowitz apartment, waiting for whatever was coming next. It had been a long time since he had been last able to go to work, and there was no point even thinking of going outside into the street. It was too dangerous. He was scared and desperate. What would the day bring? No one knew. Several members of his family had already been sent away to Transnistria. Strangely, he and his wife somehow still remained in the city. They hadn't even been removed to the ghetto, instead staying in their apartment. Apparently some mistake had been made in the records somewhere. But he was sure that the Romanians would eventually come for him. There was nowhere to run or hide. They couldn't even go out into the street.

Moses prepared a small suitcase for himself and his wife, with some clothing and a little food for the road. He only had a few bits of jewelry left, and a tiny sum of money. He hid the jewelry and the money in the folds of the clothes. He and his wife were ready. All they could do was wait.

There was less and less food at home. They economized as best they could, but inexorably their supply diminished. They felt lost and somehow indifferent, like those who know their fates are in the hands of others, that they are controlled by outside forces greater than themselves. Moses didn't know what to think or do anymore. He and his wife just sat and waited, the fear growing stronger every day, every hour. The only thing that kept him going was prayer, and Moses insisted on praying for prolonged periods every day, which helped him, gave him strength, and allowed him to support and comfort his wife.

Suddenly, towards the end of his early morning prayer, there came the sound of loud knocking at the door.

Moses quickly finished his prayer and glanced over at the suitcase. It stood by the door, ready to travel. Moses looked at his wife. Their eyes met, and there was no need for words. Tears gleamed in her eyes, but she did not say a word. They knew the meaning of that loud pounding on their door. The knocking came again, more urgent than before.

That's that, our turn has come, Moses thought to himself. Though he tried to remain calm, he felt fear getting the better of him. Not the fear of death, but the fear of suffering and the unknown. His heart pounded and he felt a little dizzy.

Moses took another look at his wife. She stood still, pale as a ghost. Moses felt wave after wave of heat, and sweat trickled down his neck.

Moses approached the door. A moment before he opened it, he peeped through the window, an old habit, and saw the head of the man who was knocking. It was a Romanian peasant wearing a fur hat, as peasants often did.

It's not a soldier, Moses thought to himself. *What could this be? Probably a robbery,* he answered himself.

He knew that if he didn't immediately open the door, the man would burst inside by force, and then he might also murder Moses and harm his wife. He fingered the folds of his clothes for the hidden jewelry, and said nothing to his wife as she stood at the other end of the room. There was no time for that — he had to respond quickly. With shaking hands he turned the key and opened the door. There was a man standing in the doorway alone, holding a frayed bag.

It's a single person, not a band of robbers, Moses thought quickly. *Maybe I can overpower him.*

The man pushed Moses inside and quickly entered, shutting the door. After it closed, Moses saw the man's familiar features but still couldn't recognize him. His wife kept standing there, frozen in place. Fear of the unknown had paralyzed her.

Suddenly Moses' face came alive. He even managed a little smile. The woman also approached their sudden guest. Aaron!

"You scared me to death," Moses said. "What are you doing here? I didn't recognize you at all. I was sure they had come to take us."

Aaron smiled and handed the man the frayed bag he was holding. "I came to see how you're doing, and brought you some food," he said.

"How do you get around?" Moses asked. "And with this hat too. You know what will happen to you if you get caught?"

"I'm not afraid," Aaron said. "They look for those who run and hide. They are not looking for me specifically." Aaron spoke in a quiet, very confident tone, as if he were the one who determined who they looked for. He only stayed for a few minutes. After Moses and his wife calmed down a little and thanked him for the provisions, Aaron left the apartment and went on his way. Moses locked the door and went over to the window to watch Aaron's lonely figure walking away.

Autumn's rose and gold came on the heels of that October. It grew palpably cold outside, and trees were aflame with fall colors as strong, cold rain fell.

Towards the end of the month, on a Sabbath, a German named Josef Elsasser appeared in the city. He was a member of the death squads, and bore a message for the heads of the surviving Jewish community. The Jewish prisoners of the Tarasivka camp on the bank of the Bug were allowed to receive parcels from their relatives. Anyone who wanted to send a parcel must hurry and bring it to the customs office. To add weight to his words, Elsasser showed a list of 106 camp prisoners, with a former Czernowitz address next to each name, the name of relatives still residing in the city, and finally the signature of each prisoner.

The remaining Jewry of the city gathered to examine the list. It was suspected at first that this might be a trap, but they had to go because the list included their precise addresses. Aaron also visited the customs office. He patiently waited his turn, and when he received the list he examined it carefully, going over each name twice. He personally knew some of those listed. He knew it was a German-controlled labor camp, and like the rest, he knew what that meant.

Aaron continued scrutinizing the names. As he finished examining the first page, he did not find his name or the name of any of his relatives. As he moved on to the second page, his heart pounded. He began to sweat. He came across more names of people he knew, people whose fates were unknown to him. Suddenly his eyes stopped on number 57: Rita Kron, Rosha neighborhood, 52. Relatives: Filipescu St. 7, Czernowitz.

It was his address. Under the name he saw a signature in Rita's hand, confident and clear. The letters were large, clear, and bold. *She retains her pride*, he thought. He continued reviewing the rest of the names on the list.

His mother-in-law Fanny was not on the list, which apparently meant that she was no longer among the living. But perhaps Fanny and Rita had been separated? Perhaps Fanny had been taken to a different place? How could he know? How could one find out?

When Aaron came home, he found everyone tense and impatient with expectation. Aaron spoke at length about the long lines, the lists, the possibility of sending parcels to Rita and Fanny. "At least we know they are alive, and where they are." Aaron was lying about his mother-in-law, of course. *I have no proof Fanny is gone*, he thought. *Maybe she's in some other place, or maybe the Germans didn't allow everyone to sign their names?* He realized he was trying to fool himself. After all, he had seen the names of couples on the list. But he really did hope that perhaps Fanny was interned elsewhere.

The families of the deported spent three days gathering whatever they could, of the little that was left. Shoes, a little soap, some winter clothes, blankets, canned food. Some women sewed threads into clothes, not because the clothes required mending but so their kin would have sewing thread. On Thursday all the parcels were loaded onto a truck parked in front of the customs building.

The authorities were generous. A Romanian customs clerk accompanied the truck to the town of Mogilev, on the border between the Romanians and the Germans. He was supposed to ensure the smooth passage of the truck at the border. The truck passed the border and disappeared into German-controlled territory in Poland.

For Aaron this was the last evidence he had that Rita was still alive. He never knew if the parcel made it to her or not. The entire story remained a mystery.

Why had the German officer shown up? Why had the Romanian authorities shown kindness, aiding in the truck's passage? What had the Germans done with the parcels? No answer was ever found.

Days passed slowly but inexorably. No two days were alike. Each was unique in the horrors that haunted it.

Since the deportation of his mother, sisters and brother, Aaron knew nothing of their fate. Nor was there any information about Fanny and Rita. Aaron tried to find something out, because he knew they were in Tarasivka, but to no avail. There were new deportations on an almost-daily basis. The Jews of the city were becoming scarcer, gradually dwindling to almost nothing. Occasionally, when another deportation was underway, the Colonel would send a sentry to guard Aaron and his family. It was good to have a guard on each such occasion, but there always remained the uncertainty as to whether a sentry would come watch over them next time. And if not, what would become of them?

It was clear to Aaron that the slightest change, like the replacement of the Colonel with someone else or German forces entering the area, would mean a turn for the worse.

CHAPTER 21

Meanwhile, the Colonel was doing all he could to retain his position, and took special care not to be sent to the Russian front. Rumors were already coming from that direction about the Russian winter and a serious German defeat. At the same time, rumors circulated that the Germans were getting ready to enter the city.

There was no telling what would happen next, and what the Romanians would do. One bright day a military unit entered the city with its own score to settle with the Jews, and the unit's soldiers went wandering through the city streets. No one could foresee what happened next. There were no clear signs. The soldiers gave the impression of being on leave, but soon enough the city turned into Hell on earth. Jewish mothers who happened to be outside with their babies were gathered on one of the bridges over the river Prut which flowed through the city, a river with deep and turbulent waters. The babies were torn from their mothers. The mothers begged, fell to their knees and kissed the boots of the soldiers and officers. Some mothers tried to fight back. Nothing helped. They saw their babies being thrown down into the river.

There were screams of despair. Women tried jumping over the bridge's railing, wanting to die with their children, but the soldiers held them back. The babies immediately vanished in the rapid waters. None survived. Even their cries were inaudible, but the despair of the mothers was heard at great distances. The soldiers were pleased with their little recreation. The officers stood apart and watched the proceedings with smug contentment. The soldiers even made sure to chase the women away from the bridge with blows and curses.

Details of the terrible incident spread quickly, and horror gripped the Jews. Even though they were allowed three hours each day to buy provisions, no mother dared venture outside with a child for a very long time.

One day a few planes suddenly streaked across the sky. They swooped across and disappeared eastward, followed by the sounds of explosions from that direction a short time later.

Aaron was in the workshop when this happened. He too heard the roar of the engines, but continued working as usual. At the end of the workday, as was his habit, he left through the camp gate. The soldiers on guard duty already knew him well. He had become part of the landscape. When Aaron passed the sentries he heard them exchange a few words. One of them was swearing to God that he had seen the planes clearly, and that one of them had had a red star on its tail rather than a German swastika.

For a brief moment, Aaron stopped short as if glued to the pavement. He recovered quickly and resumed his walk towards the house, his mind buzzing with strange thoughts.

Had he heard correctly? How had the Russians come such a great distance? Had they endured, and put the Germans in jeopardy? He didn't notice his route home. He told no one what he'd heard the sentry say. Outwardly he remained his usual self, but that night he couldn't fall asleep.

His mind was full of restless thoughts. Maybe it had indeed been a Russian plane? Maybe there was hope after all? Days passed, but no additional Russian planes were sighted. At the same time, rumors circulated that those planes had hit a certain military facility.

Winter passed and spring came. Aaron was on his way back from work, deep in thought, reflecting on the fact that several winters had passed since the madness began. As he walked not far from his home, several vehicles sped past him. At first he paid no attention, but the roar of engines emitted by more cars drew his eye. Aaron froze in place and tensed like a coiled spring. The fatigue of his workday was gone without trace as he gazed at the passing vehicles. These were no longer solitary cars, but long columns of a variety of vehicles snaking along streets, swastikas gleaming on their sides. Aaron found himself in a sea of vehicles laden with German soldiers, combatants. It was clear that they would be followed by SS and Gestapo units.

The Germans had taken over the city.

Within days they began to round up the few remaining Jews. The Germans went from area to area, from street to street and house to house, holding lists meticulously compiled beforehand. A few days later they came to the area where Aaron and his family lived. It was obvious they stood no chance. The permit given to Aaron by the Romanian Colonel held no value for the Germans.

The entrance to the building was blocked by a large, heavy iron gate which Aaron made sure to lock every night.

The night the Germans came to the neighborhood, Aaron decided to have everyone go down and hide in the building's basement. It was in the back of the building, hidden from view, so anyone unfamiliar with the building wouldn't know about its existence.

And indeed, when the night came and everyone was in the basement, the Germans showed up and began their work. They heard the sounds of soldiers approaching, and soon there was knocking on the iron gate.

Nobody moved in the basement. It was impossible to see anything. It was night outside, and even darker in the basement. It was the darkness of a tomb.

The knocking on the iron gate intensified, and soon became a barrage of blows accompanied by shouting in German: "Open immediately, this is the SS!"

The two families sat in complete darkness, holding each other, looking for warmth and comfort in each other's arms, feeling the pounding of each other's hearts and the trembling of each other's bodies. The two mothers held their babies tight, and covered their mouths so they wouldn't make loud noises. They were certain their end was nigh.

Aaron sat closest to the door. He knew that as soon they forced their way inside, they would immediately slaughter everyone, but he had long since decided that he preferred to die this way. He would not be taken to the camps, come what may. Aaron felt no fear. He wondered about his own calm. He only felt deep sorrow for his young son lying beside him. *He is only a boy who has not yet tasted what is good in life, the taste of freedom, pleasure and love. What else can I do?* he thought. Had there been another way to survive? Perhaps. In any case, it was too late to do anything about it. They stood no chance against the SS, who kept on pounding on the gate outside, their shouts making everyone shudder more and more.

The forged metal gate did not disappoint, and remained locked. In the end the Germans gave up and left. A deathly silence fell on the place. No one dared move, or even breathe. The air in the basement grew stale, suffused with the stench of fear.

The babies had apparently fallen asleep, and only occasionally gurgled. The adults stayed awake and alert the rest of the night.

CHAPTER 22

Aaron also stayed awake all night. He hadn't told anyone that earlier the same day he had added reinforcement to the gate, granting it a misleading look of neglect, as if nobody lived there. He'd made copies of the seals put on the gate by the Romanian army after the expulsion of the Jews to the ghetto at the beginning of the war.

But Aaron knew this ploy would not last very long either.

The next day was quiet. The Germans were busy with other things, except for a few soldiers who decided it was a good time to start looting. Who would oppose them?

In the midst of the looting, Aaron recognized one of his Jewish neighbors — God knew where he'd come from all of a sudden. The man was wearing worn-out clothes and a yellow Star of David on the lapel of his coat. Even without identifying markers, it was easy to tell he was Jewish. Aaron heard someone say once that the man looked like a Jewish character out of an anti-Semitic caricature.

This Jew was marching up and down the street, declaring that he intended to complain about the looting. "I'm not afraid. What can they do to me? I will complain at their headquarters," he told Aaron. Without wasting more time, he disappeared behind a corner. About half an hour later a jeep appeared, with two SS officers inside. The

Jew followed them out of the car, leading the officers to the apartment where the looters were. The officers looked like hunting dogs, ready to pounce on their Jewish victim in seconds, but they did not do so, likely simply because they had not been given such an order.

In minutes the soldiers were led out of the apartment at gunpoint by the officers. "You are German soldiers!" they roared. "How dare you engage in looting without orders?!"

They all disappeared from the street. The soldiers were loaded onto the vehicle and it sped away. The Jew disappeared in the same strange manner he had appeared. Aaron hurried back to his apartment. He was still stunned by what he had seen. How was this Jew not afraid, and able to drive the looters away? But most of all he was puzzled by the officers' behavior, for which he had no explanation.

An uncomfortable internal feeling told him something was about to happen.

But what? What could be that thing looming over them?

What else could he think of? And most disturbingly: how could he escape?

Several more days passed, but nothing happened yet. Numerous German caravans passed through the city, but they were combat units that never lingered. And suddenly there was the question: "What were all those units doing here? Aren't they supposed be near Moscow, thousands of miles from here?" The answer came soon after, from far away. It was difficult to identify precisely, but one could just guess that it was the thunder of cannon fire.

As the days passed, the cannons came closer, and at night he could see the flashes of explosions. Aaron decided the situation was getting too dangerous and that he needed to look for a different place to stay.

The next day he left the basement, his son in his arms and his wife by his side, heading for one of the suburbs. The streets were quiet and empty. Aaron couldn't understand what was going on. After many days in the isolation of the basement, they found themselves wandering through a ghost town. Aaron felt that something was about to happen.

Perhaps a curfew was imposed and I'm not aware of it, he thought. But where was the army? Aaron kept pacing, Constantine's fur hat on his head. A German soldier on horseback appeared out of nowhere and brought his mount to a halt in front of them.

Aaron looked the rider in the eye and instinctively asked in German: "Are the Russians far away?"

"You have enough time to leave the city heading westward," the soldier said, and galloped away.

Aaron breathed a sigh of relief. "I was afraid he would shoot us," he said to his wife. "But the hat helped, I think. Did you notice? There was fear in his eyes."

They kept walking a little while longer. More soldiers appeared in the distance. This time they were moving slowly, with caution, their weapons aimed in front of them, fingers on the triggers.

This is it, this is where it ends. There's no way we can avoid this. We're right in their path, Aaron thought, addressing his wife through clenched teeth: "Keep on walking, confidently, without hesitation, come what may."

The two parties came closer and closer. They could now make out the faces of the soldiers, alert and tense, weapon in hand, advancing cautiously, ready to fire, a simple pull of the finger and everyone in their path would be mowed down mercilessly. All of a sudden, for a split-second, Aaron paused to peer ahead of them once more. In a sudden decisive movement, he took out a yellow Star of David from his pocket and firmly attached it to his coat lapel.

He kept on marching straight ahead, tall and strong, until they were face to face with the soldiers of the Red Army.

The soldiers were part of the reconnaissance unit of the First Ukrainian Army.

It was an immense force consisting of many divisions: infantry, armored units, artillery and air force. They had begun a massive offensive at the beginning of March 1944, and entered the city of Czernowitz at the end of April that same year. The southern German Army Group had collapsed. Red Army forces appeared at the foot of the Carpathian Mountains, on the Romanian border.

The Red Army began to enter the city uncontested, with only a few exchanges of gunfire here and there.

German soldiers trapped in the city were shot on the spot. Russian soldiers sought revenge for what the Germans had done to them, for the murder of their families and the destruction of their cities. They were followed by rearguard units, including units of the NKVD which began to impose law and order. Now came the turn of the collaborators. All were rounded up in a short time, loaded onto trains and taken eastward. No one knew what became of them.

In the street where Aaron lived, someone reported the presence of a German soldier in one of the apartments.

A few Russian soldiers were deployed there, only to find a sick German soldier in bed. The soldier's lover, a Ukrainian woman, begged for the German's life. A short burst of gunfire put an end to the story. The Ukrainian ran after the Russian soldiers, screaming: "What will I do with him now? He is dead." Their answer was curt: "Whatever you want, what you have been doing with him until now." In the end, like the rest of those who collaborated with the Germans, the woman had no choice but to bury her German.

After the city was fully conquered, the Russians proceeded to recruit people for the war effort. Young men were taken off the street and sent to the front, or to the coal mines in the Donbas. Not many returned after the end of the war, not from the mines and not from the front.

Aaron was likewise recruited; his head was shaved, he was given a uniform, and he waited for orders. Would they send him East or West? No one knew what the choice of direction depended on.

He waited with the rest in one of the camps on the outskirts of the city, where he became acquainted with an NKVD officer who told him about the new regime. "In our country, my friend," said the officer, "you will never be able to make do with the salary you receive from the government. If you don't learn to take care of yourself, your life will be tough. If you learn to take care of yourself, you will be fine, but only if you don't get caught, because then you will have a significant price to pay."

Aaron was quick enough to understand. The two were alone together, and he had to take advantage of the situation. Aaron put his hand in his pocket and looked the officer in the eye. "I think I understand you," he said. "I think we should both be able to do alright in this city, that is, if you can help me stay on a while longer." Aaron took his hand out of his pocket and offered the officer a small object wrapped in paper. The Russian unwrapped the object, looked it over covetously, and looked up into Aaron's eyes. For a few seconds there was complete silence.

The Russian held onto the object. "Don't worry, it's a gift," Aaron said finally, "and if we stay here, there will be plenty more where this came from."

"Wait for me here," the Russian said, "I'll be back in an hour or so. I think we understand each other." The Russian put the small object in one of his pockets and marched away with measured steps. After the officer disappeared, Aaron also began to walk away. He walked slowly, deep in thought.

What's about to happen? Is this a trap? The Russian could have arrested me on the spot. Why didn't he? What is he trying to do? How will this end, and how great is the risk? Will I be sent to the front or the mines? There isn't much chance of coming back from either of those. What will become of my family? What has become of my mother, my brother and my sisters? Aaron paced back and forth in the camp, deep in thought, his imagination burning feverishly and igniting vast landscapes. Thinking as he kept walking, he didn't notice time pass. Suddenly he felt a hand gripping his shoulder.

"Where were you, damn it?" the Russian officer scolded him, having already returned. "I've been looking for you for a long time. I told you to wait there."

"I'm sorry," he said, "I had to go to the toilet urgently, you understand, probably the food."

"Never mind," the Russian said. "I am a man of honor and my word means something, and I hope you will not become a disappointment. Take this document. You are free to go home. I hope the two of us will get by just fine in this city."

Aaron stared at the document, which was written in Russian. He could actually speak Russian, but had never learned to read the Cyrillic alphabet. Despite this, he had a distinct feeling that the paper was valid, and that he was holding the key to his freedom. The two parted. Aaron confidently marched out of the camp and directed his steps towards his home. As he walked, he smiled sadly to himself and thought, *What sheer luck that I still had a gold coin in my pocket.*

CHAPTER 23

Aaron went back to work at the military shoemaking workshop, this time on behalf of the Red Army.

Part of the workforce had changed. The Romanians unsurprisingly disappeared, and were replaced by Russians, later joined by a few Ukrainians. These last were quiet people who worked for days on end without saying a word.

Among the Ukrainians, a quartet of men stood out. They had all arrived at about the same time, and were trying especially hard to work well. They looked like nice, simple people. Aaron, who excelled at human relations, got closer to them than others. During the short breaks, they would converse and eat together. Though they weren't too close, Aaron felt compelled to invite the four Ukrainians to his house, but for different reasons he repeatedly postponed the invitation.

Days passed. Aaron continued meeting with the Russian officer who had gotten him out of the camp, each keeping their side of the agreement. The Russian kept renewing the permit, and Aaron paid for its renewal as promised. The black market was doing even better than before. The risks were the same, but the possibilities were also significantly greater.

One day a military truck stopped at the entrance to the workshop, and several Russian soldiers promptly leapt out of it. They quickly surrounded the workshop and blocked all exits, their submachine guns pointed at the workers.

Aaron and the rest of the workers froze in place. No one knew what to expect.

What was this? Were they about to be killed? The soldiers were behaving like the Nazis. Aaron tried his best to think what to do, but in vain. His mind went blank. Everything had been calm and quiet only a few minutes ago.

The door on the driver's side of the truck opened. Out came a Soviet officer, red-haired and of average height, dressed in a combat uniform, gun in hand. The look on his face was one of fatigue, and his boots were covered in dust. He went into the workshop with slow, measured, but confident steps, reached the center of the floor, and stopped. He scanned the room with a blazing glare, scrutinizing each and every man's face. Aaron met the officer's gaze and felt its force, but couldn't understand its meaning.

No one dared move. Everyone froze. The officer continued to scan the people with his burning, penetrating eyes. Aaron looked away from the officer and saw the rest standing apart from each other, fear in their eyes, not knowing what would happen next. Suddenly, Aaron's gaze fell upon his Ukrainian workers. At first he thought he couldn't see clearly. But his eyes weren't deceiving him. Their faces were white as snow. Before Aaron could regain his wits, the officer motioned with his hand and the Ukrainians were taken out of the room by the soldiers and loaded onto the truck. The officer approached Aaron, faced him with a threatening expression and peered into his eyes.

Aaron returned the gaze, and felt the full force of the spirit behind those blazing eyes. Cold sweat trickled down his back, and he didn't know what to do. *Will they take me away in that truck as well? What has gone wrong?*

Their eyes met once again, and Aaron felt a subtle softening in the officer's gaze. Now the Russian officer opened his mouth for the first time, and said in a very quiet voice: "I have come on foot from very far away. From Stalingrad. And I will keep on walking and fighting my way to Berlin, if I live. In my civilian life I was a teacher. Those who were loaded into the truck killed my entire family, my wife and children. These Ukrainians were Banderites, and you gave them employment." Silence. "But it's not your fault. You didn't know who they were. You are a compassionate Jew. I have been left all alone in the world. I will take revenge without mercy because my children were shown no mercy. You don't need to be afraid of me. I will not harm you. I am a Jew like you." The officer turned around, left the workshop and got into the truck. The truck disappeared behind the bend, heading towards the forest. The Ukrainians never returned.

No one ever saw them again.

Early one morning at the end of summer, or perhaps it was already the beginning of autumn, Aaron was preparing to go to work when he suddenly heard a knock at the door. Not loud, but insistent. Who could it be at such an early hour? Members of the regime? An acquaintance? But this early? Aaron felt suspicious. He tensed up, preparing for the unexpected. He remembered the words of the NKVD officer – and what if it really was them? Who knew what they might be up to? He grew dizzy with thoughts. Aaron prepared his documents, particularly the NKVD permit required to work in the city.

The persistent knocking made Aaron hurry to the door. He approached the entrance, turned the key, and opened the door with a seemingly confident gesture. The corridor was still shrouded in semi-darkness. A lone figure stood in front of him in the twilight of the narrow space. It was a thin, short man, wearing threadbare clothes. He looked exhausted and in need of immediate help. Without hesitation Aaron took the man's hand and pulled him inside.

By the light of the door lamp, the two men stood next to each other. Staring, disbelieving their eyes, as if dreaming. Aaron dared not move, fearing the dream would dissipate.

After a while, Aaron gripped the man's arm and gently sat him down in the nearest chair, then pulled up another chair for himself and sat in front of him, very close, his hands on the man's knees as if to anchor him in the seat, to keep him from disappearing.

Little by little the man's expression changed, his tired eyes misting slightly like the slight, bitter smile of a shipwrecked survivor who had wrestled the ocean and managed to reach safety. The man's smile caused a storm of emotions in Aaron's heart.

"My brother!" He fell into his younger brother Joseph's arms.

Joseph's clothes were immediately burnt in the backyard. They were a pile of filthy, reeking, flea-infested rags, and were replaced with other clothes, too large for him but clean and warm. Already feeling better, he had a glass of tea and some food, and almost fell asleep at the dinner table. Aaron led him to a bed and covered him with a warm blanket. Joseph immediately fell into a deep, peaceful sleep, of the kind he hadn't had in years. But just before that, he managed to briefly relate his trials after his deportation from Kimpolung.

Joseph had decided to look for his older brother Aaron in Czernowitz for a reason.

Joseph, 1938

About a year earlier, while everyone was still in the Shargorod ghetto, Joseph was sent to the Trihati labor camp, on the bank of the river Bug. The Germans demanded a labor force to build a bridge for military purposes.

Together with other young men, Joseph was assigned to a group of Jews sent from Dzhurin, Murafa and other areas. They were about a thousand people altogether.

The distance from Shargorod to Trihati was very long. The drive there took eight days in a cattle train, with the car doors locked from the outside. There was no air inside, and people began to faint. There were those who did not wake from their fits, and gave up their souls. At one of the stations, while the train stood on a sidetrack all day waiting to continue its journey, a major from the Romanian army happened to be passing by.

The officer peeked curiously into the train cars. He was first put off by the stench, but suddenly realized that there were people inside, some standing up and others sprawled on the floor, given that there was not enough room for all to sit. The officer ordered the guards to immediately open the doors and windows of the cars.

"We are not allowed," the sergeant in charge of the guards said. "These are going to a labor camp, how many of them make it is irrelevant."

"Open them now!" the officer insisted.

"No," the sergeant remained firm. "We mustn't."

The officer approached the sergeant and declared, centimeters from his face, injecting as much authority into his voice as he could muster, "The military code stipulates, in the clause relating to freight trains, that it is expressly forbidden to convey any kind of cattle when all the windows and doors are closed. I will not repeat my order. Open all the doors and windows immediately, or I will court-martial you on the spot. Now! I have no time to play!" The sergeant realized he had best cease arguing with this officer. He gave his soldiers a brief order and the doors of the train cars slid open. Cool, fresh air streamed inside. Those who were still alive began to come around.

At subsequent stations, as the train waited on sidetracks, the train doors remained open. Now and then the passengers were allowed to disembark and relieve themselves. Once they used the opportunity to gather food. A cornfield stood next to the train, and they put the corn inside their clothes and smuggled it onto the train. The corn was distributed more or less equally among the men, and all who could ate freshly-picked, raw corn.

During one of the stops, Joseph was passing by one of the tracks on his way back to the train when he came across another freight train. He paid it little mind, as he was very tired and painfully hungry, and this other train did not look special in any way.

"Hey, you, come here," he heard a cry.

Joseph turned his head in the direction of the voice, and only then realized the shout had been in German, and it was coming from the mouth of a German soldier guarding the train; a soldier wearing an SS uniform.

This is the end, Joseph thought to himself, *and perhaps it's better this way*. He approached the soldier. There was a rifle on the soldier's shoulder, but he was not pointing it at Joseph.

"Who are you?" the soldier asked. "Why do you look like that?"

Joseph didn't know what to expect after a question like that. "We are workers, and we are very hungry," he answered in fluent German.

The soldier turned to his comrade-in-arms sitting in the adjacent car. "Heard that? These people are hungry. Get some food," he said.

Joseph was sure this was some kind of game, a show. No doubt they would make him pay for it. And the price would surely be high. As he tried to anticipate what might happen next, the soldier reappeared with a bag full of various food products: canned foods, biscuits and more. Joseph had long since forgotten that such wonderful things existed in the world. At first he didn't dare touch the bag, but the soldier forced it into his hands. Joseph put some of its contents into his shirt and trousers, for himself.

When he came back to the train car, the people pounced on the bag, and within seconds the contents were gone. Joseph still struggled to believe it was real, but the cans of preserves in his pockets were evidence that he wasn't dreaming.

The train began gaining speed, chugging along at a moderate pace for many long hours. Suddenly there was a deafening shriek of brakes, and the train stopped at a small station. The place was called Trihati.

Trihati was a small town on the bank of the river Bug near the city of Nikolaev, not far from the north cost of the Black Sea. The Bug had once been the border between Poland and the Soviet Union, and now stood in the way of the German army as it marched towards the Crimean peninsula, and from there to the Caucasus mountains and the oil fields within. To make it there successfully, the German army desperately needed regular supplies to secure a quick victory over the Soviets, and for this purpose a road was being built between Germany and the Ukraine, and from there to the Caucasus. The path crossed the river Bug which flowed north to south, and required the building of a bridge by the town of Trihati.

In December 1941, Himmler conducted an inspection of the southern region of the German front. He experienced firsthand the miserable transportation conditions of the existing road, which had been built by the Soviets before the war. After his return to Berlin he received the order from Hekeli to improve the road, which had been given the codename DG 4. Himmler obtained Hitler's permission to move ahead with the project on one condition: the road would be built and improved with minimal means. It was meant to last three years. Several German companies sought to carry out the task, while SS units were assigned to provide and guard the workforce. Thus the project of two thousand kilometers of road – the SS Road – was born.

Two German companies began the construction of the bridge:

Beton und Monierbau would build a thousand-meter stretch, and Krupp was to finish the remaining 500 meters. The Krupp company, tasked with constructing the bridge's metal skeleton, took the job with utmost seriousness and lent its men to it. In April 1942 the site was visited by Rudolf Wagner, the company engineer responsible for the project. Upon his arrival he received a gift: four hundred Jews became his private property for one purpose only, the building of the bridge.

An additional 1,500 Jews were transported to the site from several locations in Transnistria, like Shargorod, Mogilev and others. They were malnourished Jews who were poorly dressed for winter conditions, some of them already ill upon arrival as they began to work on the bridge. They were kept in labor camps in Trihati under the vigilant eyes of Romanian soldiers.

Like dogs, the Jews were marked as company property by means of collars which had "Krupp" distinctly imprinted on them.

At Trihati, the doors of the train car suddenly slid open. The screams of the soldiers were bloodcurdling. Joseph jumped out onto the platform, joined a long column of several hundred Jews who had just been taken off the train, and began to march while being threatened by the rifles of the Romanian gendarmes.

A neck collar worn by Jewish labor camp interns [Photo: Yad Vashem]

After a quick march of several kilometers, they passed through the gate of a camp surrounded by a tall barbed-wire fence. SS soldiers under the command of Hauptsturmführer Hekeli stood around the fence, watching over the camp. At the entrance, prisoners were counted and beaten with whips or rifle butts. A German engineer named Neumeier ordered the newly-arrived Jews to hand over all the money in their possession.

Around midnight the camp was roused by an alarm. All the Jewish workers were quickly rounded up in the camp square. Joseph was scared, trembling with fear, exhausted by the long ride and the work during the first day, with miserly food rations – pea soup that was mostly water, and 200 grams of stale old bread. He was sure they were about to be shot. Everyone stood there, silent. One thousand five hundred people stood there and waited. No one knew or imagined what was about to happen.

When Hauptsturmführer Hekeli showed up, Joseph's legs began to shake for real. He could barely continue standing. He knew something terrible was about to happen.

Hekeli and a few guards were dragging two Jews, with shackles binding their hands and heavy chains around their necks. The two were terror-struck. Their eyes said everything.

Hekeli stopped and briefly announced that the two were spies. Then he continued walking, followed by the guards leading the Jews. The moment he reached the riverbank he curtly signaled to the guards, and together they threw the Jews into the river. The two quickly disappeared beneath the surface of the Bug.

Hekeli strode back to the camp, calm and serene, and stood before the camp interns again, warning them not to speak of the elimination of the spies, or they would suffer similar fates.

The Jews were only allowed to return to their barracks after midnight. Though he was exhausted by what he had endured during the day and over the past few hours, Joseph could manage only intermittent slumber. Finally he was roused from his drowsiness by the wake-up call, the cries of the guards and the hubbub filling the frozen barracks.

Along with the other workers, he marched a kilometer and a half to the bridge-building site and set to work, trying not to stand out. During this, he overheard things, short and hurried sentences spoken in fear and suspicion. People were speaking of what had happened that night. It turned out that the two declared as spies had been working there as Romanian-to-German translators. The Romanians had brought materials for the bridge by train, and required translators to communicate with the Germans. The translators had managed to develop a connection with the Romanians working on the train, who gave them some of their home-cooked food, for a price of course. An unknown snitch informed on them to Hekeli, the camp commander, and he decided that the two Jewish workers had been spying on them.

One day a Jew left the sleeping quarters. Accidentally or not, it didn't matter to the Germans; he was shot in the head. Two other Jews were shot as well because they had received letters from loved ones interned in one of the Transnistria ghettos.

Several days of terror passed. Again the sirens came at night, and the Jews were once again assembled in the camp courtyard. Hekeli was already waiting for them. The guards brought out a Jew and dragged him into the courtyard before Hekeli, who looked at the poor man and held up eating utensils in one hand.

"Is this yours?" he asked curtly.

"Yes, Herr Commandant," the Jew replied, staring at the ground and shaking, not knowing what to expect.

With a calm, steady hand, Hekeli slowly drew out his gun and shot the Jew in the head. The body crumpled and lay there, blood streaming out in gouts. For the next few days the body remained where it had fallen, to teach the Jews a lesson.

A lesson? It was a simple story: German soldiers were allowed to send provisions back home. Among other things, they sent bottles of oil. One day a soldier noticed that his oil bottle was missing about half a centimeter of oil. The soldier complained to Hekeli about the theft. Hekeli acted quickly, checking everyone's food utensils until he found one with leftover oil. Then he got hold of the Jew to whom those utensils belonged. He did not ask questions, and did not care that the workers were starving. He knew that the Jews were there to work and die, and that he had the power to decide and do as he pleased. He was a member of the Aryan race.

Joseph was working on the raising of the bridge, along with many other Jews who had been brought to the site. Work continued through the brutally cold winter, the same winter that would overwhelm the German army, and through the searing heat of the following summer. Working hours lasted from dawn to dusk.

Neumeier the engineer had come up with a new game: in the evening, after the day's work was done and they returned to camp tired and broken, he would put a few Jews opposite one other and force them to beat each other with sticks. Woe to anyone who did not strike hard enough.

The weak disappeared quickly, and were replaced by newcomers. The food was meager. Diseases and the cold took their toll. Days passed without hope or prospects. Joseph was gradually becoming weaker and weaker, but he did his best to hold on and not yield to his bitter fate.

An additional 1,500 Jews arrived at the site. After marching about eighty kilometers without food, they were loaded onto German trucks that eventually made it to Nikolaev. These newcomers replaced those Jews who had died because of the appalling conditions, or because they had been shot. There were those who had managed to escape as well. The escapees managed to reach the Transnistria ghettos where their families were being held. But only a rare handful managed to escape.

One afternoon, Joseph saw Romanian soldiers approaching the bridge. One of the soldiers separated from the group and began to descend under the bridge, approaching Joseph. "You, Jew, come over here," he said.

Joseph had no doubts. His end had come. Only a few steps separated him from the soldier. Joseph put down his working tools, approached the soldier and quietly stood before him. He was sure his suffering would end in a moment.

Joseph remembered that that same day, after he had finished distributing water to the workers, he had sat down to rest under the bridge without the guards noticing. An old gypsy who liked to wander about the place approached him. She was an ancient wreck dressed in rags, all skin and bone, always alone. No one knew where she came from or where she went at night. Surprisingly, the Germans let the gypsy be. Sometimes she managed to talk a German guard into reading his fortune, and thus secure a larger slice of bread for herself. The prisoners in the camp took pity on her. "What future can she foretell for us? We have no future." But people liked to dream, if only for a few minutes, until the whip cracked against their back and woke them from their brief dreams.

The gypsy approached Joseph and, as was her way, began to read his fortune. He paid no attention to her and let her talk, but the last sentence she said was that he would be receiving good news that same day, and that he had a good chance of getting out of that place. The gypsy stared at Joseph's palm a little while longer, then let it go and hobbled away.

Now Joseph faced the soldier wearing a combat uniform, a steel helmet on his head. *The gypsy was right*, he thought. *I am about to be killed by this soldier. That's my ticket out of here.* Joseph did not believe in fortunetellers, but just before the end he thought maybe he should. Maybe they did foretell the future after all.

The soldier took a step closer to Joseph. "Your name is Joseph?" he asked.

"Yes."

The soldier continued. "You have a brother in Czernowitz?"

"Yes," Joseph said again.

"Were you both born in Kimpolung?"

"Yes," Joseph replied for a third time.

The soldier reached into his overcoat pocket and took out a small package wrapped in old newspaper.

Joseph's mind went completely blank. He could not understand what was going on. What did the soldier want with him? What had happened to his brother? How would he know where to look for Joseph?

The soldier looked straight into Joseph's eyes and handed him the package. "Here, it's from your brother. He is in Czernowitz."

Joseph's swollen fingers began to unwrap the package. He found banknotes and a photograph of Aaron inside.

"It's true, that's my brother," Joseph muttered.

The soldier interrupted him. "You don't need to pay me for this service. Your brother has already done that."

The soldier abruptly turned around and walked away at a brisk pace.

After the soldier had gone, Joseph experienced a strange feeling that he knew the man, but he was too tired and overwhelmed to think about it. He hid the money deep in his pocket and held the photograph in his other hand, feeling it warm his body.

The money was more than a fortune. It allowed Joseph eventually to return to his mother and sister. It was enough to buy a little food for the family. Most importantly, it meant that Aaron had managed to survive and remain in his house in Czernowitz.

Joseph wanted to keep on sleeping, but Aaron insisted on waking him early in the morning. "We are leaving to bring our family here," he said. "You will take me to where they are."

Losing no time, the two were on their way. At the Czernowitz train station, they boarded the only freight train heading east that day. Most of the trains were moving west towards the front.

They spent the whole day inside the car, waiting. Finally, when it was dark, the train began to move east: slowly at first, gradually picking up pace, finally leaving Czernowitz, moving east toward the endless expanse of the Soviet Union.

CHAPTER 24

Rabbi Shloime's wife Mindel was sitting inside what had recently been the house of a Ukrainian farmer. It was a rainy season, and the hut's straw roof provided only partial protection from the endless rain. Moisture was everywhere, in the walls, doors and windows; everything was soaked. The house was also surrounded by a field of sticky, knee-deep mud.

Mindel sat by the window and watched the road leading to the railroad. Eight days had passed since Joseph had gone out looking for Aaron, and there was still no sign of him. Her head buzzed with thoughts. War was still raging. The Germans occasionally bombed the train tracks. Besides, who knew what the new rulers were capable of?

They were stuck in this village because of the NKVD's decision that she and her children would stay and live here. All attempts to convince them or change their minds were met with sharp refusal from the officer in charge of the village. He was not open to any explanations; he had orders to follow. Mindel first tried to explain that she and her children were refugees, that the Romanians had chased them out of their home and that they wanted to return. But to no avail — this officer had orders that said otherwise.

Mindel's daughters were not at home. Due to the lack of provisions, they had gone out to work in the nearest kolkhoz so that they could bring some food home. The Germans had destroyed almost everything in their retreat. The local farmers suffered from hunger as well, and only by working in the kolkhoz could one get any provisions.

When Mindel and her children had arrived at this place on their way home, fate had something strange in store for them. They arrived with nothing, starving, penniless and with almost no strength to go on. The village was half-destroyed and most of the men had been drafted to fight at the front. They were greeted by the surviving residents, who had not been drafted due to advanced age. One of the men was the head of the village and of the kolkhoz in the area. He asked the newcomers about their place of origin, where they had just come from, and where they were headed. When he spoke to Mindel, their conversation lasted longer that those he had with others. He asked her many questions concerning the house, her husband, and the farm her family owned, as well as their neighbors in their hometown. Mindel answered his questions, and the longer their conversation went on, the more she felt that the man knew many details, as if he knew her and had even visited their home. Still, though she tried, she could not remember who this man was, sitting opposite her and showering her with all these questions. In the end, the man addressed his comrades, who were likewise wondering at the meaning of so many questions.

"You remember," the head of the village addressed them, "that when I returned home after the Great War, I told you we took a town from the Austrians in Bukovina? We met a family there who lived next to our camp. Remember I said that even though we were enemies, they treated us fairly and kindly? I have not forgotten that.

Now these people are our guests, and we will help them as much as we can, and share what we have left with them."

That same day they received a little food, mattresses and blankets, and the family was let inside so as not to soak in the rain and mud. This hut was one of the few that was more or less intact. Most of them stood charred and ruined.

Wrapped in a blanket, Mindel sank deep in thought.

She remembered October 1941. It was Rosh Hashana, and she was still at home. The grocery store was closed and everyone had gone to the synagogue to pray. That same day, after they'd left the synagogue, the authorities confiscated the family's business license because they had closed the grocery store on Rosh Hashana. Mindel did not understand what they had done wrong. They prayed at the synagogue during every Jewish New Year, with the grocery store closed. The authorities knew that and had never said anything. So what had changed? No new law had been issued regarding opening hours, so why was their license revoked?

But that wasn't all. Mere days later, the store's entire stock was looted and handed over to the Iron Guard, who controlled everything. Some of the farmers took part in the looting as well. They simply entered houses and took whatever their hearts desired.

During the Sukkot holiday, the Jews gathered in the synagogue to pray, but in reality they were there to discuss the situation. Rumors were circulating, and an atmosphere of uncertainty, pressure and fear hovered over everything. Nobody knew what was going to happen. One rumor was stubbornly repeated – all the Jews in town would soon be deported. Where? When? How? Nobody knew the answer. The uncertainty made the tension worse. Nobody could enjoy the holiday prayer, but for the moment they were all together and tried to encourage each other.

The next day, the police and gendarmes began to act. Together with municipal authorities, they marched through the streets to the sounds of drums, and loudly and threateningly announced that within 15 hours all Jews were to assemble at the train station located on the eastern side of the town's outskirts, two kilometers from the center. You could only take a few things, no more than 15 kilos per person. All had to show up, without exception – men, women, the elderly, children, babies and the sick, regardless of their condition.

In due time, the Jews of the town began to arrive at the station. There was great commotion as people darted about in distress. Families did their best to stay together. The gendarmes were already waiting and gathered up house keys. The Jews were likewise required to hand over any valuables in their possession. "Anyone who disobeys will be put to death on the spot," they were told. Cattle cars were waiting on the train tracks. The engine was billowing black smoke, ready to begin the journey.

Mindel and her children were crammed into one of the cars reeking of recent cattle transport. The floor was strewn with cow dung. Up to eighty people were crammed into each such car. They were so crowded that there was no room to sit. There was palpable fear in people's eyes. At the last moment, just before the train started moving, Mindel saw a horse-drawn cart. A sick, paralyzed man was lying in the cart, taken by the gendarmes from the hospital. The cart stopped next to one of the train cars, and the gendarmes lifted the man and threw him into the nearest car. After that they promptly locked the doors from the outside and the train went on its way.

Beside Mindel and her children stood a Jew wrapped in a prayer shawl. He had come to the train station straight from the synagogue, and now began to pray. A silence fell over the train car as the only thing heard was the prayer, the voice of a man named Ephraim. He finished the prayer and looked around him. "Be merry, my friends, it's a holiday," he said. No one smiled. It was as though they were hypnotized. No one had yet processed what was going on. No one knew where they were being taken.

The town disappeared in the distance, and the train kept speeding towards the terrible unknown.

Hours passed, and people retreated into themselves, each alone with their thoughts. Despite the cold outside, Mindel began to suffocate like so many others. The little windows did not allow sufficient airflow for so many people. The moans of the sick and the crying of babies were heard in the chilling silence, accompanied by the rhythmic rattle of the wheels against the rails.

They first reached a place called Ataki, a border town in Bessarabia (now Moldova) on the banks of the river Prut. The Romanian army had destroyed all the houses in the town. The ruins stood without windows, doors or roofs, only charred walls. The heavy smell of fire was still in the air.

The train stopped and the doors were flung open. The blind hatred in the eyes of the soldiers and gendarmes shocked Mindel. They were overwhelmed by the screams and by blows from rifle butts and cudgels. Everyone spilled out of the cars except for those who were no longer alive, whose bodies were thrown down into the sticky muck. To reach the town they had to march a few hundred meters, but the Romanians had prepared a surprise. They had dug a ditch between the train and the town, and the people had to cross over it. The other side of the ditch was steep. Water from the constant rain and snow filled the place. The Jews' possessions fell into the muddy water. Everything was soaked, as packages, suitcases, backpacks and possessions wrapped in blankets, all of which had been taken in a great hurry, now became very heavy. Many left their possessions in the ditch. They had no strength to pick them up and could barely pull themselves out of the ditch. All around them stood the local farmers and Romanian soldiers, waiting. Once the stream of people ended, they pounced on the loot. Valuables were shared between the farmers and the soldiers so that everyone was happy. Mindel and her children found shelter in a relatively large building, along with other people. They sat huddled in one of the corners, pressed up against each other, trying to warm up. The rain showed no signs of stopping, and the water trickled down into the building, making everyone wet. There was no way of escaping it.

Mindel looked around. She noticed writing in Yiddish on one of the walls, scratched with coal: "The Romanians killed us all here. Whoever comes after us, pray and say kaddish. We were killed for worshipping the Lord." Everywhere there were signs of the pogrom that had taken place. Jewish bodies lay scattered everywhere, in the streets, in the burnt buildings, in the basements where they had tried to hide, in the fields between the trees. Mindel was seized by fear. She dared not move or breathe, or look away from the soot-stained wall with the two sentences relating the story of the town's Jews. Finally she found the courage to look around, and saw they were in a building that had once been a synagogue. *What will become of us?* she thought. *The Romanians did not deport us to a different place where we could begin anew. They are driving us to our deaths, and it will take the form of horrible suffering.* The fear of death was everywhere. She did not feel the rain which was still pouring, or the cold, or the fatigue. She did not know where she was. Fear for the children became an unbearable burden, but she did not give up the glimmer of hope and began to pray under her breath, without the siddur, from memory. The cold persisted, and penetrated every part of her body. The moisture only made things worse. Hunger also began to affect her. But worst of all was the fear. Intense, crippling fear. It was impossible to think logically. There was no one to ask for help. The government was waging a war of annihilation against the Jews.

Suddenly there came a kind of whine from afar. It was difficult to say what it was. The voices got closer and closer. The whine intensified and dominated the street. A horrible sight revealed itself to the curious: hundreds of Jews, barely walking, barefoot, dressed in rags, many completely naked. The Romanian gendarmes whipped them without mercy. Everywhere a whipped Jew landed, blood would burst and drip down the tormented body. Rain washed off the blood, and the cold almost froze it solid. The faces of those people were those of hunted animals breathing their last.

Everyone who was there was moved. Someone took out their last piece of bread, another offered a little water; this person gave away a piece of clothing, that person took off their shoes, someone else gave up their last potato. Jews from the procession pounced on the food. Despite the whipping, despite the blows from rifle butts, despite the swearing and the threats, the gendarmes could do nothing. The exhausted people froze in place and no abuse would move them.

Exchanging a few words with one of them, Mindel understood that these were Bessarabian Jews from the town of Adinet, who had survived the massacre of most of the residents. They had been on the road for many days now, first driven east to the Ukrainian border, than back west to the border with Romania, then east again.

Those who couldn't endure and fell by the side of the road, into the marshy mud, never got up again.

After a while, the gendarmes managed to drive the Jews east. The whine as they approached continued as they proceeded eastward. The whipping, the groaning, the begging and the cries of pain grew more distant and faint, disappearing in the direction of the Dniester river.

A young girl marched along at the end of the procession, wearing rags that were a distant memory of the clothes that had once covered her body. She looked inhuman, almost animalistic, foaming at the mouth, staggering, stumbling, arms waving weirdly as though waving predators away. She was screaming strange things in a strange language, and occasionally released bloodcurdling cries. It was obvious the poor thing had gone mad. Before the procession completely disappeared at the end of the ruined street, one of the gendarmes approached her, lifted his rifle and aimed with perfect poise. There was a shot. The bullet struck her forehead. The girl fell on her back, arms outspread, eyes staring at the murky sky.

The gendarmes carried on their work, dedicated to the task of moving the processions along. Captain Victor Ramdan was especially active. He commanded the procession of deported Jews. He reported to and received orders from Colonel Palade, delegate of the General Staff of the Romanian Army, responsible for carrying out the deportation of the Jews. Captain Ramdan had three assistants: Lieutenant Roska Augustine, Lieutenant Popovici, and Lieutenant Popoio.

Palade initiated one of the cruelest orders: a Jew who could not continue in the procession was to be shot dead on the spot, regardless of age or sex. Many were indeed shot. The children of those who were shot continued walking. Some of them were adopted by friends, neighbors, relatives, or simply people who took pity on them. But not everyone had someone to adopt them, and this created the enormous problem of orphaned children who had lost one or both parents. But there were cases where children refused to part with parents who had just been shot by the gendarmes. They remained by their dead parents, and suffered the same fate now that their parents could no longer help and protect them.

The documents possessed by the Jews in these processions were confiscated at the checkpoints between Romania and Transnistria, and so they became bereft of identity. It was an order overseen by the leader of Romania. No records were kept, so as "not to leave traces." The only records kept by the Romanians were the group numbers and the number of people in each group.

Another order the gendarmes received was to make sure that holes for 100 bodies were dug in the ground every 10 kilometers along the deportation route, to bury all those unable to keep up with the rest and who were to be shot on the spot.

The deportation of Jews to Transnistria began on September 16, 1941, and continued until the end of December that same year. The office of the General Staff received precise information about all the ghettos and camps, and the units guarding them. General Topor headed up the office's work. The General Staff delegate in Transnistria was Colonel Palade, responsible for the executions. The orders and instructions were only given verbally. Officers who wanted written orders always received the same answer: any activity related to Jews was to be performed on the basis of verbal orders only.

On June 12, 1941, a short while before the invasion of the Soviet Union, a meeting took place in Munich between Hitler and Marshal Antonescu. Hitler revealed to Antonescu the second most important secret after Operation Barbarossa: his intent to annihilate the Jews in the conquered eastern territories.

Antonescu was brought up to speed on the forming of Einsatzgruppen and their mission as units dedicated to the annihilation of Jews. He learned about the coordination between these groups and the German army, and their methods of operation.

Following their victories against the French and the English in the West, and successful operations in the Balkans, the Germans were sure of themselves and their ability to defeat the Russians. Unlike in past wars, German forces were equipped with planes and vehicles running on modern engines, so Russia's enormous landmass – the strategic advantage that had helped it overcome Napoleon and achieve victory in WWI – was no longer a valid barrier.

Antonescu adopted the German methods, which had proven efficient in German-occupied Poland.

Government meetings were held on June 17 and 18, 1941, after which a document was issued which left no doubt as to the government's intentions regarding the Jews of Bukovina and Bessarabia. The document received the codename "Clearing the Field." Antonescu placed the gendarmerie, the army, and civilian authorities named Praetor in charge.

General Jacobovich, Commander of the Romanian army, charged Colonel Aleksandru Junescu with planning and executing the removal of the Jewish element. Operative groups were formed which incited the Romanian civilian population, especially the farmers, against the Jews. Harassment, physical assaults, looting, rape and murder were perpetrated against the Jews, who could not comprehend how the Christian population had turned against them almost overnight.

General Topor issued a notice that the gendarmerie had received special orders "to clear the field." This phrase took on the meaning of the German phrase "the final solution," and for Romanian units this meant the extermination of all Jews in the rural area, the concentration of all urban Jews in ghettos, and their subsequent expulsion.

In one of the gendarme units, an order was given to kill all Jews, including babies and the helpless elderly, because they were all endangering the Romanian nation. Close collaboration formed between Einsatzgruppe D and the Romanian army regarding the operations of the German army in territories under Romanian control, such as the city of Czernowitz.

CHAPTER 25

While villages were being purged of Jews and urban Jews were being herded into ghettos all throughout Bukovina, Mindel and her children continued their journey east. They spent long days on foot, passing Mogilev, continuing on to Azarinec and Ivaskovci, and were finally stopped at Shargorod.

There already was a ghetto in Shargorod. The entire town had become a ghetto except for one street, the only street where Christians lived.

Shargorod was a small and intimate Jewish town, with narrow streets and small old houses built with mud bricks. In the past, the town had been full of Jewish life. Its people and atmosphere inspired Shalom Aleichem to create the character of Tevye the milkman.

The ghetto was not surrounded by a fence or wall. The gendarmes weren't worried about the Jews running away because there was nowhere to run. The enormity of Transnistria meant it was nearly impossible to reach anywhere else. And should a Jew escape anyway and actually make it somewhere else, he would be reported to the authorities and face a death sentence. No investigation and no actual trial — those were the rules the Romanians set and stuck by.

Mindel, her children and the rest of the people from Kimpolung who had arrived at the town were the third wave of deportation. They were preceded by people from neighboring towns. There was no free room. The town's residents had numbered nearly 1,800 when the war broke out, and now it was crammed with more than 7,000 people. With great difficulty they found room in a pigsty, just to avoid remaining in the freezing cold, the merciless rain and wind. One critical problem was a lack of sanitation inside the house, and the lack of public toilets. For that reason the swamp on the outskirts of town became the place where ghetto prisoners relieved themselves. In the rain, in the cold, during storms, with no other option, people lost their shame and went collectively in the open. Men, women, children; shame and the need for privacy had disappeared. The swamp became a place where everyone met everyone. As they relieved themselves, they argued about every kind of topic, but especially politics. As the days went by, access became a problem. The stench was terrible and could be smelled from miles away.

Another difficulty was the lack of drinking water, to say nothing of washing. There was no food. People died daily, up to a hundred per day. The dead were buried in collective graves, in large pits. With the onset of winter and the intense cold, they encountered a new problem: the ground froze solid and became impossible to dig through. The cold reigned supreme. Mindel spent entire days scraping the inner walls free of snow, which otherwise quickly turned to ice.

Given the poor sanitary conditions, typhus broke out. There were no medications. No hospitals. Nothing to warm the houses.

Another serious problem was the orphaned children who were left to wander around alone. Thin, nearly naked, starving and sick, the children wandered the town's streets, knocking on doors and begging for something to eat.

Mindel always tried to give them a piece of bread or a potato rind. Sometimes she herself went for days without food. She couldn't understand how these orphans managed to survive. Many did starve to death, but others lived on.

There was a Jew in the ghetto with whom Mindel was slightly acquainted. His name was Ephraim Brecher, but he was likewise known by his German name Friedrich. He had been chosen to represent Kimpolung Jews in the ghetto committee.

Despite the conditions of the ghetto and the harsh winter, with temperatures of 40 below, he was not indifferent to the fate of the orphans. He and several of his friends began arranging for an orphanage. They located a suitable house in bearable condition, outside the ghetto but within town limits. There were ten rooms in the house, where they sheltered the children they'd gathered from the streets. Ephraim brought together around 180 weak, hungry, filthy children, dressed in rags and crawling with lice, suffering from various diseases, and began to care for them. The orphans were given room and board, a clean piece of clothing, a little food and even medical attention from Jewish doctors in the ghetto. There was no running water in the house. Members of the team carried buckets of water from far away, despite the terrible cold and deep snow. Ephraim and his men surpassed themselves when they managed to organize warm meals for several hundred more half-orphans.

The orphanage's kitchen worked almost non-stop to manage the feat. Meals were served twice a day. One of the most important features of the orphanage was the warm attention lavished by Ephraim and his team on the children bereft of fathers and mothers.

The physical and mental state of the children began to improve somewhat. This allowed Ephraim to begin preparations for classes. Children were divided into groups by age. They were given a little paper Ephraim found in the building, and the school year began. The children studied Romanian and Yiddish, reading and writing, the Bible and even Zionism.

Mindel wondered how they had managed to set up an orphanage outside the ghetto. Where did all the provisions come from? She wondered, even though she knew the answer. The ghetto prisoners were aware of how easily tempted the Romanians were by "baksheesh" – bribes. They had inherited the word from the Turks, under whose rule they'd lived for centuries, with the meaning of the word remaining the same throughout the ages.

The head of the ghetto committee was Dr. Teich, who had previously been the head of the Jewish committee in the city of Suceava, the district town of Kimpolung. Dr. Teich had much experience in dealing with Romanian authorities. He knew their mentality well, and understood their codes of communication, excelling at developing close contacts. Thanks to the ties he'd developed with the ghetto authorities, he got in touch with Bucharest's Jewish Rescue Committee and asked for help. The letter he sent made its way from Shargorod to Bucharest in the pocket of a Romanian officer on holiday. The letter detailed the unbearable living conditions in Shargorod, and asked for things that were required to ease the suffering there.

The Rescue Committee and relatives who had remained in Romania responded immediately.

Clothes, medicine, food and a little money were delivered to the Shargorod ghetto. The quantity was not great, but it would certainly do as a first response. Subsequent deliveries came more frequently and helped save many lives.

The ghetto formed a committee to manage those who were interned, and to find ways of improving the living conditions. Each community, formed according to their settlement of origin, chose between two and three representatives, twenty-five in total.

At first, when the Jews had only begun to arrive, they would organize according to the city or town they'd come from. The differences were significant. Kimpolung Jews managed to open a tiny store where they sold cheap items, given that the people of Kimpolung had been robbed of their possessions on their way to the ghetto. Czernowitz Jews arrived in disorganized groups and were left without any support at all. Deportees from another city were able to open a bakery, and sold cheap bread. Another group organized a soup kitchen that was able to serve close to two hundred people.

Everyone soon realized they had a shared interest in organizing life in the ghetto, and from there it was only a few small steps to organizing a shared committee.

One of the first authorities the committee formed was a Jewish police force. Fifteen in number, they would patrol the streets of the ghetto, with a band on their sleeves and sticks in their hands. A Jew named Dr. Koch, from Kimpolung, who had previously served as a reserve officer in the Romanian army, was chosen as the Chief of Police. They were charged with two functions: first, to maintain order inside the ghetto, and second, a much more complicated, painful and controversial function, up to the very end of the war, and perhaps forever: to send people into forced labor, by an order determined by the Jews themselves.

The Germans demanded a workforce on the other side of the Bug. Rarely did anyone return from there. The men chosen for this labor often ran away or resisted, and thus the forced and violent rounding-up of laborers was done by the Romanian gendarmes. In addition, Romanian authorities demanded that work be done in Shargorod. Sometimes laborers were paid trivial sums for this work, which was considered less difficult. Thus laborers for these tasks were chosen by the Jewish police, without Romanian gendarmes. They thought it would prevent the Romanians from taking over the ghetto, and create a situation where the gendarmes interfered less and less in the ghetto's internal affairs. But for many, this function of the Jewish police remained a source of emotional trauma that divided the community.

Everything was not entirely negative – help came from an unexpected source. Ukrainian government officials from nearby kolkhozes supplied provisions without the knowledge of the Romanian authorities. A local miller of German origin secretly supplied Jews with flour, and even went to the trouble of making the mill kosher for Passover. Inside the ghetto, a kitchen was opened to serve food for those in need. At first it served around two hundred meals a day, and in time the number rose to fifteen hundred per day. The bakery also increased production, and within a few months it was able to satisfy the needs of all ghetto residents.

In the spring of 1942, there was another outbreak of typhus. Shargorod had a small hospital with 25 beds. The limited number of beds made it impossible to attend to all who needed treatment. The committee oversaw the organization of the hospital, and raised the number of beds by 100. The Jewish doctors from the ghetto and sanitation workers did their best to battle the epidemic. Towards summer, the epidemic was contained, but despite these efforts more than half the people who contracted the disease did not survive.

Midway through 1943, a large shipment of medicine arrived from Bucharest. This shipment enabled the establishing of a pharmacy in the ghetto. Most of the medicines were handed out free of charge, though some were sold at low prices. The committee also built a small agricultural farm meant to supplement the food with additional vitamins so lacking in the ghetto.

But the committee did not stop there. Disinfection rooms were created, as well as a public bath, and the town's power station was restored. The station was comprised of several engines which ran on diesel. Electricity was restored, and as a result so too was the water supply. In addition, a small factory was erected, a workshop producing soap for ghetto residents. Some of the soap was sold to Ukrainians from nearby villages. The ghetto's sanitation department installed public toilets and made sure they were emptied and cleaned on time. The risk of disease dropped significantly.

Shipments of money kept arriving from Romania by means of couriers, who charged a fee of thirty percent, though sometimes the money would disappear before it arrived in the ghetto. But there were also extraordinary occurrences. There was, for example, a family from Kimpolung who had run a business with a Romanian partner before the war. When the Jewish family was deported from the town and the business was entirely handed over to the Romanian partner, the latter managed to locate his Jewish partner and regularly sent money, paying the fees for delivery. He did so all through the war. The money helped the Jewish partner survive, saved him from hunger, and eventually allowed him to return to town at the end of the war.

After the material conditions of the Shargorod ghetto had improved, the committee applied themselves to the next task. They received permission from Romanian authorities to open the town synagogue. Prayers were conducted on a daily basis, and even marriages were held there. In the autumn of 1942, a prayer was conducted in memory of the 1,500 victims of the ghetto.

In time, Shargorod Ghetto became the most organized ghetto in Transnistria. Many Jews from different ghettos found shelter there, even though it was strictly forbidden to move from one ghetto to another. People snuck in, changed identities and integrated into the community. The gendarmes made no special effort to search, because of the presence of the Jewish police. The Romanians stayed out of the ghetto's internal matters.

Some of the ghetto residents hid local partisans and even provided them with food, despite the severe shortage. When the Red Army approached and the Germans and Romanians began to retreat, strong suspicions arose that the Romanian and German armies might slaughter anyone still alive in the ghetto, as they had done in other places.

Partisan units entered the ghetto, determined to defend those interned there.

Despite the improvement in the conditions of the ghetto Jews, by the time it was liberated by the Red Army in 1944, only half of the 7000 Jews originally held there had survived.

On October 16, 1942, at 11:00, a Transnistria expo was held in Bratianu Square in Bucharest. Among those present at the opening were the deputy leader and his wife, ministers, members of the Romanian government, public figures, diplomatic representatives, Romanian journalists and representatives of foreign presses, members of the German military delegation in Bucharest, and many others. The central pavilion of the exhibitions was decorated with Romanian, German and Italian flags. A 400-voice choir performed nationalist songs suited for wartime. Giant representations of Marshal Antonescu, Hitler and Mussolini were hung in the most prominent places.

Priests opened the ceremony with a prayer for the leader's health, and the success of Romanian soldiers in their fight against the Russian Bolsheviks. The occasion was the anniversary of the conquest of Transnistria.

After the religious ceremony was over, Prof. Gheorghe Alexianu presented himself before the distinguished audience and opened the exhibition with a speech. He explained that the exhibition was tangible evidence of the war, and the incumbent duty to wage a military campaign to destroy the Red Army, which until very recently had posed a threat to all of Europe. The war was a wise cultural measure taken to preserve the foundational institutions of Romania and the entirety of Europe.

The exhibition was tangible evidence of the fact that Romania had answered Hitler's call to join the defense of Europe, as well as Romania's achievements in restoring life to Transnistria after its destruction at the hands of the Soviets.

Not a word was said about the deportations of hundreds of thousands of Jews, Romanian citizens, to ghettos, and their deaths due to forced labor in camps throughout Transnistria. The exhibition demonstrated achievements in agriculture and industry, as well as a sales center for agricultural produce.

Prof. Alexianu, who had the honor of opening the grand event, was the governor of Transnistria, and a professor of law at several universities in Romania, including the University of Czernowitz. He was considered a talented administrator and a friend of the Prime Minister, appointed to the post by Antonescu himself.

Alexianu came from an Armenian family that had fled Turkish rule in the 19th century, due to anti-Christian persecution. The family came to Romania and did well enough to become respectable Romanian citizens. The professor himself was a known anti-Semite who had been given his post because of his views. He was a member of the Romanian government and took part in the decision-making, including all matters concerning Transnistria. The fact that his own family had been refugees fleeing the terrors of the Turkish regime did not impede his activity against the Jews.

In decree number 23, Alexianu was appointed governor on

November 1, 1941. He began to organize Transnistria so as to take control, especially over the Jews. The region was divided into thirteen counties, each ruled by an appointed official with a deputy in each sub-county.

The Romanian gendarmerie was responsible for organizing Jewish forced labor. The gendarmes would take Jews by force from streets and houses, beating and robbing them in the process. The commander of the gendarmes in Transnistria was Colonel Brosteanu, eventually succeeded by Colonel Mikhail Iliescu.

Gustav Richter, Eichmann's delegate to Romania, reported to his superiors as follows:

> Ion Antonescu, the leader of Romania, made the decision to gather 110,000 Jews from Bukovina and Bessarabia (Moldova) along the Bug river in order to exterminate them. The government of Transnistria was charged with the task. To carry out the order, the local government was provided with gendarme units and units from the occupying Romanian forces. The end goal was to clear Transnistria of any Jewish presence. Meanwhile, labor camps and ghettos have been built to house the deported Jews until spring, when conditions will be available to deport them east of the river. The governor informed the commanders of the Fourth Romanian Army that one thousand Jews would arrive each day to join the fifteen thousand already in Transnistria. At the end of the process, one hundred and fifty thousand Jews will be deported. We hope that by spring of 1942 the conditions will be right to deport them east of the Bug river so that all of Transnistria will be free of Jews.

On November 9, 1941, the gendarme commander Vasiliu reported to Antonescu that the current stage of deportation was over. A total of 108,200 Jews were in Transnistria. This was not the end of the deportation, of course. In the coming months, and the following year, many more trains would arrive.

CHAPTER 26

Mindel vaguely remembered the endless journey. She remembered the constant march through the freezing cold, the rain and snow, with barely any food. She remembered people collapsing. People being shot. People falling into the river and disappearing. She remembered whippings, the blows of rifle butts, and especially the terrible humiliation of being transformed from a free human being into a hunted animal. But she did not remember details. She did not remember who else had left the town with her.

She remembered only those who remained alive. She was too tired to remember. The exhaustion began to overwhelm her. She remembered being ill with typhus and losing consciousness, and when by chance she came to, her son Jacob had already passed.

Mindel remembered her husband's words a short time before his death: "People will wander the streets and not know where they belong and what they are to do, people will lose their homes and identities."

What else is in store for me? Will I ever return home? she wondered. Mindel woke up to the reality of the cold room. The entrance door was flung open and a man burst inside. His sudden appearance interrupted her train of thought and brought her back to her miserable wet room. A tall, robust man stood in the doorway, dressed in clothes which were half-civilian and half a Soviet military uniform. He wore boots and a visor cap. At first she thought it was the village officer, but the next moment she came to her senses and recognized the man – her elder son Aaron, with Joseph behind him.

Aaron held his mother in his arms for a long time. Mindel didn't even have the strength to cry. She wanted to, but couldn't. After she calmed down, Aaron uttered a single sentence: "I came to take you home." He already knew about the NKVD officer's decision to not allow his family to return home.

An hour later he stood in front of this officer and introduced himself.

"I am an NKVD worker in Czernowitz. I have been sent to this area to look for raw materials, leather, for the workshop." Without hesitation, Aaron took out a document and handed it to the officer. The officer examined its contents. The document confirmed Aaron's words in exact detail.

"There is nothing left in this place," the officer replied, "and I doubt you will find what you need."

"I have found my family here, and I intend to take them home with me to Czernowitz," Aaron went on.

"That's impossible. My orders say they are to remain here."

Aaron knew arguing would not help. "I understand. I will sleep here tonight, and tomorrow or the day after I will go back to Czernowitz. I will check the village in case I might find something for the workshop after all."

Aaron wandered the village accompanied by Joseph, who had already gotten to know the villagers. He did not care about the leather. He was looking for a way to take his family with him.

After several hours, the brothers returned to the shack where the family was waiting. Joseph returned first, and Aaron came later. The sisters were home. Their mother had already told them of Aaron's arrival, and when he came in, they welcomed him with great excitement. But there was no time for sentimentality. Aaron told them to prepare for the trip that very night. They all went to bed early that evening, but no one was able to fall asleep. Past midnight, everyone was awake. They dressed in layers and went out through the rear window of the house into the night – quietly, so that no one would notice. Aaron led them away from the house and the main road. After walking for a while they reached a grove on the outskirts of the village. There a villager waited atop a horse-drawn cart.

Aaron addressed him: "I suppose you remember what we agreed on. You are to take us to the ferry and get us across the river before dawn. Once we are on the other side of the river, you get your pay."

It was pitch-dark, without a star in the sky. The road was on a level plane. Neither Aaron nor the others knew the way. The only choice was to trust the local man driving the cart. But Aaron was uneasy. *What if the farmer reports me to an officer?* he thought. *Several years in a prison camp is the best I can hope for. And what will become of my family?* Thoughts chased each other in his head. The cart, meanwhile, continued creaking through the dark. The farmer kept encouraging the horse as it struggled to pull the heavy cart through the sticky muck.

The farmer wanted to earn money, and his greed was stronger than the officer's orders. The cart kept moving west, and in a few hours they reached the riverbank where the ferry awaited, built from thick logs bound together. A long, thick rope was tied to tree trunks at opposite ends, across the river.

Jewish refugees stood by the ferry, waiting to be transported to the western side of the river, but the ferryman refused to take anyone who was unable to pay the fee. Without hesitating for a moment, Aaron began to barter. In the end, the refugees were taken to the other side. Only after the last of them crossed the river did Aaron and his family board the ferry along with the cart, the driver and the horse. The ferry slowly detached itself from the eastern bank and began to move away from the shore. The dark was near-perfect; you could hardly see the silhouettes of the passengers. The waters were turbulent, the stream was strong, and the night was cold, but Mindel did not feel the chill. She sat in the middle of the ferry, wrapped in an old, thin blanket unsuited for the weather conditions. She clearly remembered crossing this river in the opposite direction, before the onset of winter, when it was a lot colder. The waters had been turbulent then as well, even though they were close to freezing. She remembered soldiers pushing people into the river, how they disappeared amidst the waves and eddies. She couldn't understand why the soldiers did it. Their uniforms reminded her of her son, who had served in the same army. The Romanian army that took her son had also chased her out of her house, to a faraway foreign country. This same army had pushed people down into freezing waters.

Later, when they were already far from the river and much time had passed, an insistent rumor began to spread among Jews that some of those who had been pushed into the river belonged to a group of young people who had made it to Turkey, where they found help and reached Palestine.

Suddenly she remembered again the words of her husband, Rabbi Shloime, shortly before his death: "People will wander the streets without knowing where they belong…" How had he known that, and why hadn't he been understood? Back then no one knew, and couldn't understand what he meant. *Had we understood, we could have gone to America, where my brother lives.* Remembering her brother, she felt the wonderful taste of hot boiled potatoes in her mouth. The taste was so real that without noticing, she began to make chewing motions. She could see her farm clearly, the fruit trees hanging heavy with apples and pears, and in the distance the cherry blossoms. The furrows of the vegetable garden, with onions, cucumbers, and the green dill plants. When the season was right, she would use the many cucumbers in the garden to make pickles, with lots of dill, garlic and salt. She knew the right proportions to lend the pickled goods their fine taste. She would put the pickles into small caskets and jars, and store them in the cellar.

This cellar was a real cornerstone of her household, and served as a refrigerator in the summer. It stored all manner of edible goods, especially those which could spoil in the summer. During especially hot days it always felt good to go down into the cellar, where it was pleasantly chill. You could rest a bit from the heavy heat while working comfortably, preparing food and storing it. During winter, the cellar stored a lot of the family's food.

The potatoes lay there, covered by a thin layer of earth. Thus they could be stored for longer, lasting almost all winter. The other vegetables were stored in similar fashion. In the winter, the cellar was always warmer than the outside. Frost and ice never formed down there, and the food never spoiled. When Mindel was busy down in the cellar, the children knew she was not to be interrupted. The place was important to her. It contained the food for the entire family. During the long, cold and snowy winters, if anything was missing in the kitchen Mindel would go down into the cellar to bring what she had stored there beforehand.

Her lands stretched all the way to the edge of the forest, up the mountain. When the government decided to build a road across their land, between the house and the forest, Rabbi Shloime decided to sell the plot next to the forest. With the money he earned from it, he built a nice addition to the house. This new structure had two stories, and he built a beautiful new porch on the front side, with wooden carvings decorating not only the new part but going all the way around the house as well. This new structure was meant for one of the daughters, for when she'd grow up and get married.

All at once Mindel came out of her deep reverie. At the same moment she realized she was sinking, along with the ferry. *Who knows what will become of us and where we end up next?* she thought. *What does it matter anymore? We are sinking, and everybody knows that no one comes out alive from this river. Here we are stuck in the middle of nowhere, and the hostile rushing water is claiming its due. Perhaps I have always been here, and the rest was just a dream? How can we get back to the farm? Maybe this boy Aaron knows the way, maybe he will know how to bring us back to the farm.*

Mindel knew they were drowning, and didn't know what to do. She could see Aaron's outline at the front of the ferry. There was another outline beside him, probably the ferryman. They were both holding the rope tied to the other shore and pulling with all their might. She heard Aaron groan with the effort, and everyone who was able to help was doing their best. "Don't give up!" Aaron shouted. "Pull with all your might! We are close. The road home is on the other side!" His voice was commanding and confident. Despite the darkness, Mindel felt the ferry being swept away, but Aaron and the others did not let go of the rope and kept pulling.

A sudden strong blow almost knocked them all off the ferry, which was now almost entirely underwater. Aaron held his mother. "Quick, we are at the far shore," he said. "Let's get off, we must go on." He was breathing hard. It was apparent the strain had been enormous.

When they reached the western side of the river, the ferryman got his pay. The cart continued to the nearest town's train station. The driver got his due as well. Without saying a word he turned his cart around and disappeared from the station. There weren't many people at the station. Who would want to go west? That was where the front was. The west-bound trains were frequent, and they only had to wait a few hours.

For a sum, the station master stopped a freight train loaded with soldiers and equipment on their way to the front. He also knew the train had a short stop at Czernowitz. The train stood at the station for a minute and a half, long enough for Aaron and his family to get into one of the cars. Only then did they notice that it was dawn. They found room for themselves in one of the corners, all huddled close together, trying to warm up. There were Russian soldiers in the car, asleep and unaware of what was going on around them.

Mindel put her head against the side of the car. Despite her great fatigue, she couldn't fall asleep. Only after a while resting like this did she realize she was soaked through, and so were all her children. They had still not dried out from the ferry. Exhaustion got the better of all of them. Her legs were beginning to hurt, but she had grown used to it, knowing there was no cure, and only the hope that she would see her farm again made the increasing pain bearable. *At least my legs did not freeze the way they did when we crossed to the eastern side a few years ago,* she thought. It was winter then, and like today she had gotten wet crossing the same river. After crossing, they had covered a lot of land on foot. She couldn't even remember how long the march was, but once they reached a resting place, she was unable to take off her shoes.

They had frozen solid.

The children had to take the shoes apart in pieces, saving her legs at the very last minute. In fact, the long march had saved her legs because the effort helped retain some heat in them. The socks were soaked and close to freezing as well. They massaged her feet until they warmed up a little, put a pair of children's socks on her and managed to find a pair of shoes among the things they had brought with them. They were too large, but they were dry. She looked at her children on the floor of the train. They were all on their last legs, and the rocking motion of the train put everyone to sleep. *It's so they can stop worrying for a bit and sleep,* she thought. Her son Jacob was not with them. He'd contracted typhus during the first winter after they arrived at their place of exile. In fact, everyone had contracted it, including her.

The doctor from their hometown had not been able to do anything about it. He'd had no way to help, and the only thing he could do was state people's time of death. Everyone had a fever. She remembered Jacob covering her with a coat. She recalled nothing else. She came to after several days of hallucinations with Jacob no longer beside her. The day after he'd covered her with his coat, his temperature had risen and he had succumbed to delirium, never regaining consciousness. Jacob had been buried deep in the woods, together with many others. The soldiers wouldn't even allow anyone to mark the grave.

Strange, that she should suddenly remember the day of his death, as it had been told to her.

The 1st of May, the Russian worker's holiday. This boy had served in the Romanian military too. He had worn their uniform. His friends, his comrades in arms, had objected to his grave being marked, Mindel thought. She looked at the Russian soldiers sleeping close by. Their uniforms were somewhat different than the ones Russians had worn in the previous war, but they had the same Slavic features. Back then they had been the enemy. She remembered an incident from the previous war, after the Russian conquest. A Russian soldier, who had apparently been a farmer before he was drafted into the service of the Tsar, went into a cowshed, tied a rope to a cow and began to lead her outside. Mindel ran after him, screaming for him to give back the cow, that she needed its milk for her children. The soldier tried to chase her away, but she wouldn't let go. He kept pulling the cow after him. Mindel chased him, screaming at the top of her voice: "Give back my cow!"

This continued until a Russian officer happened by and stopped the soldier. "What are you going to do with that cow?" he asked.

"Take it home," the soldier said.

"Do you know how far you are from home? And when will you get home, if at all? Give the cow back to the woman now. She has small children at home who need the milk." The soldier handed the rope over to Mindel. He looked very disappointed, but submitted to the orders of the officer. She held the rope firmly, turned around and led the cow back to the shed.

Today the Russians are not the enemy, Mindel thought, *so why didn't they allow us to return to the farm? Why wouldn't they permit our passage?* She had no answer and could not explain this behavior.

After several hours of thoughts and memories, before she fell asleep, she remembered Aaron's words just before they stepped off the ferry onto the shore: "There on the other side is the road home."

CHAPTER 27

The train continued on its way west. The smoke from the chimney was thick and black, covering all the cars being pulled by the engine. The smell of smoke penetrated every car, and it took time to get used to it. But the important thing was that the train was going west to Czernowitz. After a day and a half on the road with almost no stops, the train stopped at the Czernowitz station.

It was possible to breathe now. Almost the entire family had made it.

Aaron's brother Jacob had not survived, and did not get to come back home. He was buried far away in Transnistria, in an unknown spot.

The damned war was about to end. The front line was now far away. The war was being waged deep inside Germany, apparently very close to Berlin. It would be a matter of months or even weeks before it was over.

The first signs of spring appeared in Czernowitz. Snow was melting and the first flowers were peeking through the white mounds. The Russian Communist regime was very rigid, and they were still in a state of war.

Aaron decided that he had to return with his family to Kimpolung. He wanted nothing to do with the Communists. He had to return to his hometown. But it was impossible at the moment. On the other hand, the more time passed, the more difficult it would be to return. Those who left had not done so of their own free will. They were people the regime had designated as capitalists, and after their property was confiscated, they had disappeared in the east and no one ever heard of them again. Others who tried to leave without permission were soon caught, accused of all kinds of strange crimes and thrown in jail.

The borders were closed. The railway tracks were broken, and it appeared that going back to the farm was not possible, at least for now. But Aaron's instincts said otherwise. The longer he stayed there, the more difficult it would be to leave later. It was impossible that everything was sealed. There had to be some way. One only had to know how to look.

Days went by. Aaron became the manager of the NKVD workshop, and it was obvious they needed him to keep running what had become a small boot factory for the Soviet army.

But Aaron had learned that nothing was certain under this regime. A small mistake was not forgiven. If you fell from grace in their eyes, your prospects were grim.

Aaron was determined to return to his hometown. But how? Meanwhile he spread a rumor among the neighbors that he intended to move to one of the city suburbs, to live in a bigger house, because his mother and sister were living with him. Everyone thought it made sense, and got used to the idea of Aaron moving out.

There were even people who showed interest in his apartment, hoping to move in once Aaron left.

One day Aaron loaded the few belongings he had onto a cart drawn by two horses. Then the family climbed in. Aaron said goodbye to the neighbors, gave them his new address, and promised to stay in touch. Of course he first had to organize his home and take care of his family. To make time for moving, he asked for and received a day and a half off from work. He promised to return and make up for the absence by working longer hours.

Aaron locked the apartment's front door and slid the key into his pocket. He told the landlord he would be back tomorrow to pick up his remaining possessions.

The cart began to move in the direction of the new suburb. After moving north for some time, once they were at a considerable distance from the apartment, the cart suddenly changed direction. Now they were moving south.

The cart kept going for the rest of the day with few stops, and only towards evening did it leave the main road and turn onto a side road. After about half an hour they reached a clearing in the woods, where a lone abandoned farmer's hut stood. Everyone went inside to get some rest and stretch their limbs. Their legs had fallen asleep from prolonged sitting in the cart. The driver tended to the horses, watering and feeding them, and only then joining the rest of the group at the dinner table. The meal itself was meager and mainly included bread and a little cheese. There was no time to cook. And it was dangerous to light a fire, lest someone notice.

After eating, the driver addressed Aaron. "From here on out the way is unfamiliar to me. What's it going to be? What do you intend to do?"

"I know the way from here," Aaron said, "trust me." Aaron did not know the way, but he knew how to proceed.

It was completely quiet, and the darkness was almost total. Everyone was silent, and when someone had to speak, they whispered.

They sat in silence, eyes getting used to the dark until they could begin to make out the surrounding area. A ruined fence lay on the ground not far from the window, and some distance away a forest stood, so dense that even in the daytime no human eyes would be able to penetrate further than a few murky meters. An hour later, a figure suddenly appeared out of the dark. The man stopped right next to the trees at the edge of the forest and stood there, completely still. Aaron left the hut and went as far as the fence on the ground. There were no more than a few meters between them. The figure advanced towards Aaron, and they met over the remains of the fence.

They shook hands.

"We're all set to move on," said Aaron.

"I'll have some water, and then we move out," the man replied. "It's a difficult and dangerous road. Hopefully we will be on the other side by morning."

He approached the well behind the house, pulled up a bucket full of fresh water, and drank his fill. "Let's go," he said curtly. His voice was quiet and reassuring. Though he only uttered a few words, there was something about the way he spoke that radiated confidence.

Everyone was already on the cart. The man climbed up as well, took the reins in his hands and urged the horses to move, and the cart disappeared into the forest thicket. It was obvious he knew the way well. Despite the darkness, he behaved as though it were midday.

The man was a young fellow of about twenty-five, with a lean yet robust body. His hair was light brown and smooth, combed back and cut short in military fashion. He had smiling eyes that bespoke good nature and confidence. Despite his perpetual and beguiling smile, he was a determined man who did not give up on any goal he set himself.

His name was Saul, but he was known as Sashka. Aaron knew him from Czernowitz. He had lived there with his parents before the war, a normal Jewish kid.

When the Russians conquered the city for the first time in 1940, Saul was about nineteen. Before he and his family knew what was going on, Saul was drafted into the Red Army and sent far away. He made it to the Manchurian Chinese border, where the Red Army was preparing to repel a Japanese attack. A few months later his unit was sent to the Polish border. There, in a foreign country far from home and amidst people he had barely gotten to know, the war overtook him.

Operation Barbarossa had begun. The Germans attacked and advanced east with lightning speed. Germany had violated its non-aggression pact with the Soviet Union. The German army crossed the border into the Soviet Union without warning, launching an attack of enormous power. Like many other Soviet army units, Saul's unit found itself cut off and surrounded. Many were taken prisoner or died, but Saul's unit had other plans. They would fight, trying to reach their forces no matter what. They would do everything possible to rejoin the Red Army forces. That was their decision. So began a long and dangerous journey east, a handful of soldiers desperately trying to make it out of a German trap.

At night they followed the German army east. During the day they rested in hiding places, occasionally raiding small German units for food, weapons and ammunition. Along the way they became expert at these raids, especially when it came to hiding their tracks and choosing routes of egress, so that the Germans would have a hard time locating them.

Saul was an essential part of the group because he knew German, thanks to which they knew the locations of both the German and Soviet forces. With the help of the information Saul was able to obtain while sneaking into German camps at night and listening in on soldiers talking, the group was able to determine the direction of their search for Soviet forces. Fighting their way, less than half the group finally managed to get through and rejoin the Soviet forces. They were immediately added to another unit and continued fighting while retreating east for several months. One day Saul's unit reached a very large and wide river, with a great city on its banks. Saul noticed the large number of Red Army soldiers, most of whom were busy raising fortifications.

"Here," said the unit officer, "there will be no more retreating. We will make a stand here and stop the Germans no matter the cost."

This was the first time Saul had heard a command other than retreat. He was very tired. For months he had been fighting without stopping. Nevertheless, he liked the new situation. *No more retreat,* he thought to himself. *I hope there will at least be enough weapons and ammunition here.* He looked around. It was getting dark. A cold wind was blowing from the east and it had begun to snow. The first snow of the year.

Saul turned to the soldier next to him. "Where are we?" he asked. "What do you call this city?"

"Stalingrad," the soldier said. "That river you see is the Volga."

Saul had never heard of the city before, but he was familiar with the river and even knew where it flowed. Only when he realized where he was did he understand how far he'd come from the Polish border. He had crossed this vast distance on foot, while fighting. He didn't know the hard part was still ahead of him.

Saul fought in that campaign, no longer thinking of retreat. There was no time to think of anything but the fight against the Germans, the terrible cold and the hunger. How to get more ammunition and another bit of dry bread, perhaps another tin of canned meat.

The fight itself went on everywhere, in every dugout position. Within the city they fought not only for every house, but every floor of every house, sometimes every room.

Good God, Saul thought, *since you have sent me here and given me a weapon to hold in my hands, let me make the best use I possibly can of it. I want to make it back home.*

The Jewish kid from Czernowitz became a war machine, mowing down Germans.

He never fired in bursts. He adopted a personal method of aiming and shooting, firing single bullets and hitting most of his targets. This also allowed him to economize on his ammunition, which was scarce.

Saul and what remained of his group had a pair of German uniforms, and on more than one occasion they barely managed to put them on in time to survive. Saul, who knew German, could tell what the Germans were up to based on their shouts, which often kept him alive. Many in his unit were wounded or killed, others took their place and were wounded or killed in turn, only to be themselves replaced by others. More than once he heard bullets whistling past his ear, but someone up above was keeping watch over him.

He clearly remembered the first major attacks against the Germans. The Red Army amassed large numbers of soldiers and threw them against the German army. Line after line of soldiers went in waves against German machine guns. Usually only the first line had rifles. The wave that followed the first would carry on with the charge, despite the hellish fury of machine gun fire. They would pick up the guns of the fallen and charge onward until they fell as well, when the soldiers of the third wave took their place, picking up the same rifles again and carrying them a little further.

Despite the slaughter, the soldiers kept charging and never wavered. Thus the first important German position was conquered since the beginning of the war. Russian losses were heavy, but surprisingly no one complained. There was even a kind of irrational happiness. Every time Saul finished this kind of charge, he remembered the officer's words: "There will be no more retreating, we will make a stand here and stop the Germans no matter the cost." The officer himself had long since been killed by a burst of German bullets.

After a while, food supplies improved and they began to receive warmer clothing, and most importantly they were all stocked up on weapons and ammunition. Saul could have been wounded in any charge he joined, and perhaps rest for a while in some field hospital. But it was in vain. He kept on charging. His friends running next to him were killed and immediately replaced by others, but he remained unscathed.

At first he asked himself how this was possible. He repeatedly asked himself the same question, and would give the answer himself: "I don't know, that's just the way it is." There was no time for reverie. The German counterattack was at its peak, followed by another Russian charge. He continued the cruel fighting until he saw the German soldiers of Field Marshal Paulus with his own eyes, surrendering with their hands in the air amid their own dead, freezing by the thousands in the snow of February 2, 1943.

Saul remembered the start of the battle, which began on November 19, 1942. The Sixth German Army under Field Marshal Paulus was fighting to conquer Stalingrad, and almost succeeded. Most of the city had been conquered, and fierce fighting was taking place, but Stalin had issued a single command to the Red Army: not one step back.

The Third and Fourth Romanian Armies were sent to aid the German army in the region. Under German command, the Third Army positioned itself in the bend of the Don River, on the left flank of the Sixth German Army. Its mission was to protect the left flank from attack by Soviet forces. The Fourth Romanian Army positioned itself to protect Paulus' right flank.

The Red Army launched their attack early in the morning when the territory was covered in heavy fog, which limited the visibility of Romanian outposts to just a few meters. Copious mortar shells rained down on Romanian positions, with a fury never before seen. The earth shook as if an earthquake were taking place.

Before the soldiers could regain their senses, T-34 tanks rolled out in massive numbers to attack the Romanian armies. Following the tanks were thousands of soldiers, breaking the defenses of the Romanians, who collapsed under the pressure of the attack. The Russians understood that the Romanians were the weak link in the German defense, as they were not appropriately armed despite Hitler's promise to supply them with German weapons. They were spread across a large territory and it was clear that they would not be able to defend themselves. Indeed, after only a few days of fighting, the Russians surrounded Paulus' Sixth Army, along with what remained of the Third and Fourth Romanian Armies, large portions of which had simply been swept away during the attack. Of the approximately 250,000 Romanian soldiers flanking the Sixth German Army, 150,000 officers and soldiers had been killed, wounded or simply disappeared. The Germans and Romanians found themselves surrounded by the Red Army. This time it was Hitler, the German dictator, who gave the order not to retreat, to fight to the last bullet. When the last bullet was gone, and the last piece of bread was gone, and thousands more had been killed or froze to death, when there was no hope left at all, Paulus surrendered. Those who survived began their long road to captivity, from which many would never return.

The Germans blamed the Romanians' disloyalty as the cause of the defeat. The Romanians blamed the Germans for not equipping them as promised, and for disregarding Romanian warnings of an attack being organized that would threaten both armies.

A deep rift formed between the allies. The soldiers of the Third Romanian Army were also taken into captivity by the Russians.

Lieutenant Gregorii Andrei was one of the Romanian officers who described the event. His memories have been preserved in the archives of Radio Romania:

> On the day of the surrender it snowed heavily. We marched in a long column of five hundred officers. It was difficult to walk because of the snow and the storm. The column kept getting longer. We ate walking, whatever remained of our food. Russians on horseback with automatic weapons guarded the column. After a whole day of marching we were allowed to get some rest in a warehouse that had been broken into. We stormed inside. There wasn't room enough for everyone, half of us were left outside. I was so tired I fell asleep immediately. In the morning we were kicked awake.
>
> Not everyone got up. Some froze to death. We kept on moving. We got more and more tired. The hunger was increasingly intense. I and a few others sat down to rest. We heard shots, saw guards shooting at people who had sat down like us. We got up and moved on. Fear gave us new strength.
>
> After a very long march, we finally reached a freight train. 40 prisoners per car. We received food: a little bread and very salty fish. No water. The doors of the cars were locked from the outside and we were on our way to the unknown. We received no medical attention during

the ride. Occasionally the guards asked if there were any corpses in the car. There were many. The guards divided the cars into two sections: the dead on one side and the living on the other. We arrived at the Ornaki prison camp. Life in the camp was very difficult. In winter the temperature dropped below 35 for a very long time. There was little food. The work was backbreaking. Many got typhus and died. The camp also held German and Italian prisoners. All had the same problems. Dozens died daily.

Because of the intense cold, you could not bury the dead. The earth was too frozen. Piles of the dead waited for thaw in the spring, when deep holes were dug. The dead were thrown in and covered in lime and dirt. There was no sign left to indicate the burial site."

So the soldiers of the Third Romanian Army, who had conquered Czernowitz and Bukovina, and had gone to war against the Jews on the orders of their leader, got a taste of the death marches, the helplessness and hopelessness, the hunger, the diseases, the executions. The Russians did not spare them, just as the Romanians had not spared the Jews.

Did the prisoners of the Third Army reflect, while in captivity, on what they had done to the Jews?

During those years they did not try to resist their captors, despite being a disciplined and experienced army.

Saul later learned that the campaign had taken the lives of more than a million Soviet soldiers, and about eight hundred thousand Germans. Saul continued to fight, but was now advancing west, with the Germans in retreat. He kept going like that until the end of the war. He learned many military roles: saboteur, paratrooper, patrolman, radio operator, a translator questioning prisoners in the field, and a signaler. He was always a combatant, always on the front lines.

After his unit entered the city of Prague, he finally stopped fighting. He and his friends were left there as a garrison force. After four or five years of fighting, Saul was the only survivor of his original unit. He had no way of contacting his family and knew nothing of what had become of them. He convinced his commanders to let him go to Czernowitz to look for his family. They were convinced, and he was discharged from the Red Army.

He never found his family. He had nowhere to go, so he began using his military experience to take people where they wanted to go, under the very noses of Soviet soldiers who were barring people from returning home.

The cart kept creeping through the dark, with Saul holding the reins. He was taking them down a very strange path, now turning right, now left, now seemingly retracing his route. He did so over and over again. The passengers completely lost their sense of direction. They couldn't tell if they were going north or south, right or left. But Saul did not hesitate for a moment. He directed the horses confidently and only stopped once or twice to let them rest.

When he stopped and got down from the cart, he signaled to Aaron and the driver to sit tight, disappeared among the trees and returned after a while. When he came back he said curtly, "We can go on." He got back on the cart, gripped the reins again, gave the beasts a lash and got going. Only he knew where he had been.

So the strange journey continued through the night. The passengers fell asleep now and then, but were woken up soon after by the swaying cart or the branches of a tree whipping across their faces. Slowly the dawn came. The treetops were swaddled in mist and covered with dew. With daylight the wind revived as well.

When it was morning, Saul stopped the cart by a stream. "We can rest here a little," he said. "The border is far behind us. You are now in Romanian territory, being Romanian citizens, and besides, nobody's going to ask you your business here. This is a defeated country and there are other refugees returning to their homes." Then he pointed and added: "Continue along this path for about three more hours and you will reach a road that will take you to your city. My duty is done here. Don't worry, you will have no trouble finding your way."

After a short rest, Saul got to his feet, said goodbye to everyone and disappeared into the forest in the same strange way he had appeared. He moved confidently, without making a sound. Not a single dry twig cracked under his feet. Though he moved slowly, he disappeared in a blink and everyone knew he would never be found. Surely he had already changed directions several times over.

CHAPTER 28

Though they were tired, they did not linger long. After two hours the cart was on its way again. This time the driver was back in the seat, holding the reins and lashing the horses. Just as Saul had said, the cart emerged from the forest after three hours and stood on the side of a road leading into Kimpolung.

It was an old unpaved road that wound through the mountains. The way was muddy and the wheels of the cart kept jumping in and out of potholes, fragments of mud spraying in all directions. Sometimes it rained, as was the norm for this time of year. The rain constantly refilled the potholes, soaking the cart's passengers.

But time was short. They had to make it to the farm.

There was a pleasant feeling of not being on Russian soil anymore. It gave them confidence, and they believed they would soon be home.

Aaron sat by the driver and gazed forward and to the sides. Mindel, wrapped in a blanket, sat in the middle of the cart, surrounded by the others who were similarly trying to warm themselves up, their heads bobbing to the rhythm of the cart. The driver kept urging the tired horses onward, but what mattered was that they were getting closer and closer.

Who knows what's there, Mindel thought. She remembered the Iron Guard looting her possessions. But strangely she could not remember what happened afterwards.

Suddenly she remembered her husband, Rabbi Shloime. She didn't know why he came to mind now. Maybe because she'd been thinking of Saul. The boy had already seen much. It was a miracle that he was still alive. He must have been fated to survive. She remembered that Saul's war story had ended in Prague, in Czechoslovakia. This reminded her that years ago, her husband had ordered a siddur from Prague. It was a handsome prayer book that had served Rabbi Shloime on a daily basis. For years the rabbi never parted with it, not even for a moment. In time the pages of the book became thinner and yellowed, especially at their lower edges, where they began to fray.

What became of that siddur? Surely it ended up in the trash or was used by Romanian soldiers for packing paper or worse.

Mindel was angry with herself for not remembering what had happened to the siddur. Since Rabbi Shloime's passing it had always been in its usual spot, serving their sons during prayer and always returned to its place afterwards. Perhaps she didn't dare ask about the book because she was afraid of bad news. None of the children mentioned it. Perhaps there was no opportunity to do so. They had barely managed to survive, after all.

The closer they got to the house, the more she worried about the siddur. Thoughts of it wouldn't let her be. It was all she could think about, as though the rest of their problems had already been solved and everything had returned to normal, with only the book left to make things perfect. She kept imagining its fraying yellow pages and what the rabbi used to write at the bottom. She saw before her the words in Yiddish. Something very important, concerning family events. She saw the letters so clearly and knew they were familiar and of the utmost importance, but despite her best efforts she could not decipher them.

Mindel fell asleep. Fatigue got the better of her. The rocking of the cart, the rain, the proximity to her home – nothing could keep her awake. She sank into a sleep deeper than any she'd had in years.

It was very early. Still no sign of sunlight. Kimpolung was asleep. Even the farmers, the earliest risers, were still asleep. Aaron's cart entered the city from the east and slowly made its way west, homeward.

Aaron took the cart along the main street. Despite the darkness and the years that had passed, he saw that nothing seemed to have changed. The houses which were so familiar were still there, as before. Not even one new building had been erected. There to the left was the elementary school, and opposite it the house where Fritz's relatives lived. At the edge of the city was the town jail. The further in he went, the more familiar the sights became. The houses of friends and acquaintances from the past, most of them now gone — who knew what people lived there now.

The cart passed the courthouse, then the public garden, the town's green heart. The chestnut trees which had grown for years in the garden stood tall in the morning's chill air, observing the passing cart.

Between the trees he could make out a small pool with little animal sculptures, mouths gaping to shoot jets of water that almost reached the tops of the chestnut trees. A little way past the pool stood that same old rotunda of polished wood. During warm summer afternoons an orchestra would play music for the garden's visitors. And if it rained, as it often did, most visitors would seek shelter inside, waiting with the band for the sun to come out. Often one could see a rainbow with amazing and thrilling colors.

A little further off was the town's magnificent church, rich in beautiful colors and gold leaf, especially prominent on sunny days. Close by was the German church, built in an entirely different style – more somber, white-walled, and smaller in scale compared to the other more colorful church.

They saw one of the alleys leading to the train station. Nothing had changed. Everything seemed as though they had never left. The intervening years and what had happened since had left no visible sign on the face of the town. Everything was frozen in place, time had stopped, and Aaron felt as if he had just been here yesterday.

They approached the town hall. It was a handsome Austrian-style building, with decorative window frames in front and on the sides. Behind it, on the hill, stood the new synagogue, the Temple. Aaron remembered Moses Rubin, the town's impressively active rabbi. He had only been thirty when elected Rabbi of Kimpolung in 1922. His abilities and talents spoke for themselves. He was chosen by a congress of Jewish communities in Vienna, together with twenty-three other representatives, to join the council of Torah sages in the international Agudat Yisrael. In Kimpolung he was also on the Red Cross council. But his main concern was teaching the children Talmud, for which he had brought a teacher from Transylvania. He organized a charity fund to care for the poor, and also cared for several communities in neighboring towns where there were no rabbis at the time.

The Temple was not the only synagogue. Not far from it stood the old synagogue, and in the yard stood another which served as a Talmud school. There were two smaller synagogues as well, open mainly on weekends, one in the eastern suburb and one in the western part of Kimpolung. There was also a mikveh in the town.

Aaron remembered Yankel Schechter, the famous cantor of Kimpolung.

In addition to religious activity, the town had had an active Zionist community represented by almost all possible movements: Poalei Zion, Klal-Yisrael Zionism, the Mizrachi, the Revisionists. The veteran organization was "Theodore Herzl," founded when Herzl was still alive, and many of Kimpolung's Jewry were enthusiastic adherents. And of course there were youth organizations: the Shomer Ha'tzair, Beitar, Bnei Akiba, and the Noar Tzioni. Many of Kimpolung's women were energetic members of the Women's International Zionist Organization (WIZO), active in the fields of culture and society.

The cart was approaching the other end of the town, and from there it was not far to their house. They passed the Christian cemetery, which rekindled a memory of an event which had happened years before the war. One night, after midnight, Aaron had been on his way home after a night out in the center of town. As he approached his house, he saw startled people returning to the town. He recognized one of his neighbors crossing himself as he ran, praying in Romanian. Aaron stopped the man, who looked scared and confused.

"What's happened, neighbor?" Aaron asked, concerned.

"Half an hour ago I was on my way home, and imagine, as I was passing the cemetery I saw a demon. He blocked my path. Danced about and made strange, scary noises. Nothing to speak of, probably the ghost of one of the dead had the hankering for a walkabout tonight."

Aaron found it hard to believe. "Neighbor, could you have had too much to drink, to make you see what you think you saw? Because you know no such thing has ever happened in this or neighboring towns."

"I tell you I saw it clearly. I'm sure I wasn't dreaming. And so you know, I didn't have a drop of drink all day. Don't believe me, do as you please, but don't go through there tonight. I am going to pray." He disappeared quickly in the direction of the church.

Aaron hesitated at first, but his curiosity got the better of him, even though he was not superstitious. The cemetery was right there, but he saw no sign of anything resembling what the neighbor had told him. Aaron smiled to himself, and while wondering what had scared the neighbor and the other people who'd fled the place in such a commotion, he found himself in front of the cemetery. He had been through this place many times, at all hours of the day. It was serene.

Suddenly a horrible shriek split the night. Aaron was startled, and before he could regain his senses, he saw a strange figure leap out into the road, reaching a height of around three meters, hovering there. The figure in white landed nimbly in the middle of the road and faced Aaron. He tried to go around, but the figure blocked his way, performing a strange dance in the air and making eerie sounds indeed.

"Should have listened to the neighbor," Aaron murmured to himself. "I could have spent the night in the center with one of my friends. Why did I have to get involved with this strange thing?" But he was already thinking of a solution. He approached the side of the road, took hold of a plank from a wooden fence and, gathering all his strength in one decisive motion, he managed to yank out a piece of wood. The figure was getting close, jabbering monstrously. Aaron swung at it with all his might. There was a horrible thud. The makeshift cudgel split into pieces and Aaron was left with nothing in his hands, but the figure had split as well. The terrible sounds stopped, and instead he heard human laughter from the other side of the street. Emerging from the cemetery he saw several young people about his age. They were locals studying in Bucharest, having fun on vacation. They took their fun seriously, having built a rag doll wrapped in white sheets. The sheets flailed in the wind, lending the figure the appearance of a ghost. They had stretched some ropes from one side of the street to the other, tying them above the trees and splitting their group in two. The teams positioned themselves on both sides of the street and pulled the ropes so that the figure came to life and struck horror into the hearts of simple city folk, until Aaron's blow put an end to the grim entertainment. Aaron recognized the fellows and burst out laughing. They ended up going back to town together, celebrating the incident till early morning.

"Just so you know, no one could pass the cemetery tonight," one of the young men told Aaron on their way home. "You are the only one who dared face the demon. How did you find the courage?"

"It scared me at first, but I don't believe in demons. And though I saw the figure prance about, I noticed at some point that the sounds weren't coming from it, and had the idea of taking a swing at it," Aaron said.

Aaron remembered his Romanian childhood friends growing up together in the town. What had become of them all? How many of them had served in various positions in the Romanian army? Which of them had taken part in the deportations? Which of them had killed Jews?

It was around four in the morning and the town was still dark. The cart came to a stop next to Rabbi Shloime's house, the house where Aaron had been born. He looked at it. Nothing had changed. It looked a little neglected, but it was all there. The windows were shuttered, the door locked. Aaron approached the front door and tried to open it. Meanwhile, everyone had climbed down from the cart and were waiting for Aaron to open the door, but it was locked from the inside. Aaron rattled the handle in disbelief. He tried to pull it open, but in vain. He lost his temper. There were intruders in his house. He didn't try to think of any tricks — no time for cleverness. Without regard for the consequences, he was going to enter his own house even if it meant breaking down the door. He showered it with kicks and blows, making the house shudder.

"You in there!" he shouted. "Come on out! Come out or it won't end well!" He looked terrifying, covered in sweat from effort and anger.

His fists were bleeding, but he paid them no mind. He wanted to be inside his house.

Mindel looked at her son. She had never seen him like that, as if in a fit of madness. He was fighting that door with a fury he hadn't known he possessed. She wanted to calm him down, but he would calm himself once the door was open. He wanted to get back what had been taken from him, what he had been robbed of.

There was a great crash. Aaron had almost kicked the door in. He was preparing for another blow when the door opened from the inside. A couple of farmers from the neighboring village stood in the doorway.

"We received the house from the government two years ago. We were told to live here…" they mumbled, but when their eyes met Aaron's they bit their tongues. There was no point in any further explanation. Words were irrelevant.

"We will just get a few things that belong to us, and we'll be out," said the woman. Aaron entered the house, barely containing his fury. He was ready for anything, but once inside he began to calm down. The couple left as quickly as they could and departed for their village.

Everyone went inside and stood in the middle of the room, looking around, scanning every nook and cranny, not quite believing their suffering was over. They were home.

Yes, it was their house, but it was almost completely empty. All their possessions had been taken. And yet their house was standing, and they were inside.

They sat on the floor. The exhaustion and tension had taken their toll.

Aaron went out to the cart, and brought down their few possessions with the driver's help. Aaron paid the man and the cart turned around to go back where it came from. After he brought their things inside, Aaron went to look at the vegetable garden, and the cherry and apple trees in the backyard. The trees stood tall in the dim morning light, waiting to be cared for.

Aaron's gaze wandered to the larger yard. On the other side of the fence stood a neighboring house, the house where Constantine lived.

Without hesitation Aaron walked up to the house. He was about to knock, and only then noticed that his hand was bleeding. He hesitated a moment, then knocked anyway.

"Who's there?" came a male voice.

"Friend," said Aaron. "Open up, I want to talk."

Aaron recognized the voice of the neighbor, Constantine's father. "Wife, I think I hear Aaron's voice, open the door."

The door was immediately opened. The old man stood in the doorway, his wife behind him. He looked at Aaron and pulled him inside. "You must be hungry," he said.

"I'm not alone, we're all home."

"Woman," the old man said, "the neighbors have come back, prepare food for everyone."

The woman got a fire going in the oven, prepared a generous amount of mamaliga from maize flour, and brought an assortment of cheeses from the cellar and eggs from the coop. When all was ready the two families sat down to eat a hot home-cooked meal, the kind they'd been used to before the war.

Constantine's father continued to feed them for months afterwards, until they were able to manage on their own.

The next day, after Aaron had gotten some rest, Constantine's father approached him and said, "Come, I have something to give you." The old man took him behind the cowshed, moved a few planks aside, took a hoe and began to dig. Suddenly the hoe struck wood. The old man stooped down and dug with his hands, Aaron helping him. They unearthed a small chest. From within the chest, the old man removed an object carefully wrapped so that moisture wouldn't get inside. He handed it to Aaron.

"Here. I know this is important to your mother. Just before they were deported, your brother Jacob was here and asked me to keep it until you came back."

Aaron took the parcel and returned to his house. Mindel was sitting by the window, the way she used to before, to rest a bit from household chores while looking outside. But this time she was sitting on a blanket spread on the floor, gazing at the empty room. In this room Rabbi Shloime had received guests. It was the largest room in the house, and as he built it he was probably already thinking of it as the large room for the many guests who would come through the years. Aaron sat down by his mother and handed her the package that had just been dug up.

"The neighbor kept this for us, he was given it by Jacob just before the deportation," he said.

Mindel took the package, looked at it for a long moment and began to unwrap it carefully, in case there was something precious inside.

Peeling off the final layer, she saw Rabbi Shloime's siddur. The familiar old siddur. Those very frayed pages with the rabbi's clear handwriting, his occasional marginalia. Mindel gestured to Aaron that she wished to be alone. He respected her request and left the room. It was the only time he saw his mother weep.

When Aaron was gone, Mindel looked at the siddur again. The hard black binding was most frayed at the bottom left, where her husband would turn the pages. The color had faded somewhat, but the letters were still legible. Mindel made them out with ease.

At the top, in large black lettering, the cover said "Siddur".

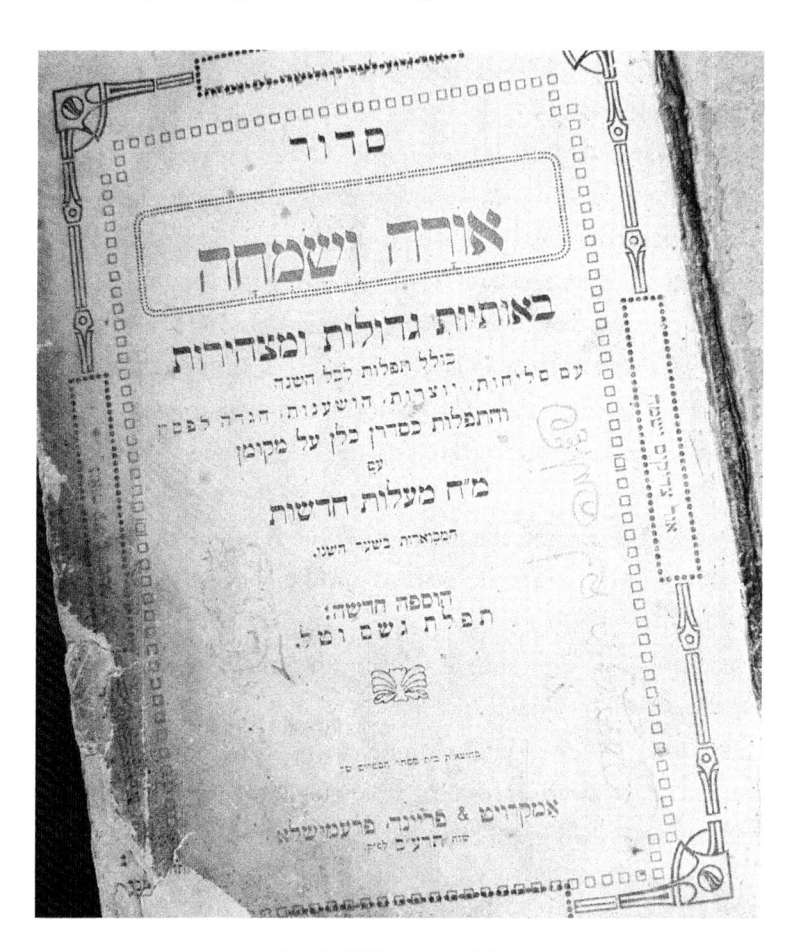

Rabbi Shloime's siddur

Below that, inside a black frame, bold red letters declared:

Light and Joy
including prayers throughout the year with slihot, yotzrot, and hosannas,
the Passover haggadah, and seder prayers in their entirety
with a compilation of new virtues.

A bit below that, the page said, "new edition." These words were also printed in red. Below them were the words "prayer of rain and dew" in black print.

Mindel carefully leafed through the siddur, one page at a time — at first without reading, as if she wanted to check that all the pages were in place, that none had been lost. Then she reached one of the notes written by her husband. Without letting her eyes linger on the handwriting, she read the words of the siddur: "We have sinned, forgive us, Creator; Hear O Israel, the Lord is our God, the Lord is One; Blessed be the Name of His glorious kingdom forever and ever; the Lord is our God, the Lord reigns, the Lord reigned, the Lord will reign forever."

Mindel kept turning the pages until she reached another handwritten comment at the bottom of another page: *Joseph, died 21 Heshvan 5678 (1918).*

God Almighty, she thought. *This must have been my father. All these years I never remembered him.*

Her father had died while Mindel was giving birth to her baby. She hadn't been aware of his death. No one in the family had wanted to tell her until she'd given birth. Her father was buried in his village that same day. Mindel, of course, could not take part in the funeral. After the baby was born, healthy and strong, she was told of her father's passing, and Mindel called the baby Joseph in his memory.

Joseph was the youngest boy in the family. Mindel never bore any more children afterwards.

After she had gone over the entire siddur page by page, she continued to sit alone, praying and weeping, her husband's book in her hands.

Mindel stayed in her room for the rest of the day. She allowed herself moments of weakness, but was unwilling to share them with others. She left the room as evening came. Her face showed she had been weeping a lot, but her eyes were dry now. Her gaze was as everyone remembered, a half-smiling look of kindness, but older and more tired.

Aaron studied the people in the room. He looked at his mother, his wife, his infant son sleeping in one of the corners, his brother and sisters. They were home. It was empty, yes, but they were all there.

The cowshed stood empty in the yard. The fruit trees and vegetable patch awaited.

It wasn't much, but it wasn't nothing either. *We need to begin anew*, he thought.

CHAPTER 29

It was a wonderful Sabbath morning on the West Coast of the United States. Everyone woke up later than usual; it was almost ten. A calm and pleasant weekend on the Malibu coast of the Pacific Ocean.

When the guest came down to the living room, he found Irving sitting in his favorite spot by the bar. Despite the early hour, he was holding a glass of white wine. Irving looked deep in thought.

The ocean was still misted over, and the shore was covered in seaweed spewed onto the sand during the night's tides.

Irving noticed the guest and bid him a hearty good morning, accompanied by a big smile. The girl and the two women came down as well, soon filling the room with laughter and good cheer. After fifteen minutes or so they sat down around the kitchen table, where they were served a rich breakfast and a variety of drinks, though they mainly preferred the wonderful fruit salad.

After the meal came the visitors Irving had invited in honor of his guests. The living room and inner courtyard filled up with people. Wine was served aplenty, and around noon everyone sat around a long table outside, under a few parasols. The atmosphere was pleasant, and lively conversations flowed.

The girl went down to the beach, where she busied herself building sandcastles.

Later, after the last of the guests had departed, Irving and the guest went down to the beach. Jessie the dog joined them at a brisk trot. Jessie was a hunting dog with sleek brown fur, a young lightning bolt of energy. Her long ears rippled in the wind as she dashed around. When she encountered neighbors on the beach she preferred to join them, despite her owner's cries calling her back. In the end she was tied to a leash and they kept on walking.

"You know," Irving said, "in the thirties we lived in New York, and when Father went to visit his sister in Kimpolung, we kids didn't know any of this. Mother told us nothing, and we had no idea where Dad had gone for two months. One day we woke up and he wasn't there. Mother said we had to be patient. Dad never actually explained why he kept the trip secret. Only when he came back did he tell us he was visiting his sister."

They kept walking leisurely along the beach. "Your father was a warm man and cared greatly about his family," the guest said. "You remember he tried to convince Aaron to come here with him? He thought Aaron would get settled and bring the rest of the family over. Your father apparently had already thought to be careful with the immigration authorities back then, until he saw how things were going. In any case, Aaron had other plans and went to Czernowitz.

"But Uncle Louis had another reason to visit Kimpolung. His elderly mother was still living alone in a neighboring village. She was too old to hear of moving anywhere, so your father arranged a pension for her via some bank. He transferred the money from here month after month, until the day she passed away. Luckily for her, she died at home before the war broke out. But your uncle Yakl, your grandma's brother, wasn't so lucky. He lived next to your grandma in the same village in Zhadova. He was married and had a daughter named Mila, a beautiful girl. She was about twelve when the three of them were deported from the village. They ended up in a small village in Transnistria called Fejerat. The conditions there were particularly inhuman, and they didn't even last a single winter. Joseph, Aaron's brother, tried looking for them, but it was in vain. Only a year later someone from that village told him that the three had died while looking for scraps in a trash heap."

They kept on walking. The ocean waves slipped across the sand, almost touching their feet. Irving was the first to speak. "I can only applaud my father leaving his place of birth and coming here. He was just sixteen when he came here, and managed to do well on his own.

"We were financially secure. I studied at university and have no reason to complain. I was lucky not to have been born in eastern Europe. Why didn't Aaron want to do the same? I think he would have been able to do well here."

"Aaron never explained his reasons for doing things to anyone, not even afterwards. The fact is that even after his return to his hometown, he never thought of going anywhere. He organized a large shoemaking shop, hired workers, and the business flourished. But not for long. As you know, the Communists took over the country. The shop was nationalized and Aaron once again became the head of the city's shoemaking business, now the property of the government. A business he'd built with his own hands."

Irving peered at the horizon. "Was there any contact between Aaron and my father after the return to Kimpolung?" he asked without turning his head.

"The year after they returned, there was a terrible drought in Romania. People died in the streets because of hunger. The situation in Kimpolung was slightly better because it was a mountainous region with plenty of streams and small farms. One day Aaron was urgently summoned to the post office in the center of town, where he was given a note he had to sign. He received a huge parcel with American postmarks on the wrapping paper, and he was almost certain he recognized your father's handwriting. And indeed, when he came home and opened the package he found a letter from your father. He wrote that he'd managed to locate the family with the help of the Joint, and that he was sending some initial aid. He hoped the package would reach its destination, and once he got an answer, he would send more. The package included canned food, powdered milk, and other foodstuffs that helped them through the drought, when it was difficult to find provisions. The package also included winter clothes, which were also a blessing, because winter was looming. Aaron replied in a long detailed letter. He described what had happened during the war, who had survived and who hadn't, and of course he thanked your father for the package. But no more packages came. Occasional letters did, and Aaron answered them."

"I know," Irving intervened, "my parents, especially my mother, did their best to gather things to send. We helped pack things, but all the packages ended up coming back. Romanian authorities did not allow such mail to reach its destinations anymore. After several tries, my parents began to send only letters. The letters got through, I gather, since they did not come back and were answered."

"That's right," the guest said, "only the letters got through. The Iron Curtain had begun to descend upon eastern Europe, but back then no one knew that was the name of the game."

"Yeah," Irving said, "I guess that's when it began. I think you need to write a book about this whole story, the family history during the war, the ghetto, Transnistria."

"Why?" asked the guest.

"Because no one knows the story," Irving said after a pause.

Kimpolung today

CHAPTER 30

The day the guests had been awaiting expectantly finally arrived, and early in the morning they were already out, happy and excited. The guest and his wife reclined comfortably in the back seat of Irving's gorgeous Mercedes. The girl sat between them, leaning her head against her father, who put his arm around her. The car slid along the shoreline with a smooth rustle, and from there headed east along the highway towards Anaheim. While the rest of the passengers gladly gave themselves up to bubbly chatter, the guest's mind was wandering through other worlds. From his seat he saw Irving's smiling profile above the wheel. *The comfortable life in the States is so different than ours in Jerusalem*, he thought. *Irving and his wife seem so serene. How is life determined by a single choice made decades ago, at a junction where one decision determined the future?*

We are both descendants of a single family which began its life journey in the Austro-Hungarian empire of East Europe. Uncle Louis immigrated to the U.S. looking for a better future. The family members who remained survived the first World War, at the end of which their citizenship changed and they became citizens of Romania.

The second time the family split was in 1940, right after the Molotov-Ribbentrop pact, when the city of Czernowitz where Aaron and his wife Hermina lived was annexed by the Soviet Union, while Kimpolung, where Mindel and her family resided, remained in Romania.

Two significant changes took place soon after. The first was in 1941, when the Romanians took back northern Bukovina, and the Holocaust of local Jewry occurred. The second was in 1944, when the Soviets retook the territory and regained control of Bukovina.

After the war Joseph tried to illegally make Aliyah to Israel, but was captured and imprisoned in Cyprus. When the state of Israel was founded, Joseph was among the first immigrants, and immediately upon disembarking from the Aliyah Bet boat he was recruited into the army and participated in the War of Independence.

When the war was over, Joseph opened a grocery shop and delicatessen in Jaffa, and being very likable, he was known among many by the fond name Yossileh. Food buffs came in droves from all corners of the city to savor the special pickles he made in large barrels, and various delicatessen specialties which reminded them of the tastes they'd enjoyed in their youth in Romania. Yossileh had two sons: the elder was named Jacob after his brother who had died in Transnistria, and the younger was named Benny.

Grandma Mindel arrived in Israel when she was almost eighty, together with Hilda and her daughter Esti, Yossileh's sister, who also settled in Israel.

Briti, Fritz and Erna's daughter who had escaped the ghetto with Aaron, likewise survived, made Aliyah and is living in Holon with her two children Ilan and Dana.

Like many Jewish families, we live in many places around the world. Some of the Holocaust survivors chose to settle in the United States, South America and Australia, and some have even chosen to resettle the cursed lands of Europe. Most came to Israel after the war.

Mindel in her nineties, Israel.

Over the years, many chose to leave. But for me, Israel is my homeland, I never had nor will ever have another home, though we had to cower in armored rooms as protection against rockets, and though terror attacks are the norm in Israel as a whole and in Jerusalem specifically. Sometimes when our enemies rise up against us, I ask myself if I have made the right choice, whether my decisions were still right for my family and especially my young daughter. But how can you ever know what will happen in the future?

You can't. Back then, in Europe, we had integrated into society culturally and economically, we were loyal to the nations where we lived and made our contributions to society, and we were sure those were new times for us, when we would no longer be second-rate citizens but equal among all other nations.

And what has history taught us? We found that our sense of belonging was an illusion, that culture was but a thin layer over primitive, barbarous feelings, and that anti-Semitism is a phenomenon just waiting to rear its ugly head.

So in spite of everything, there is but one place for us Jews, the one and only place in all the world. It was not for no reason that generation after generation prayed "next year in Jerusalem." Jerusalem always was and will forever remain the apple of our eye.

Family members who live in other countries may enjoy better material conditions, but reality may turn on them at any moment, the way it happened to our parents. But in Israel, our country – the Jewish state – we are the masters of our fate here, free to defend ourselves. In Israel no one will look down upon us, we will never bow or hide. We are here, in the land of Israel. Our land. No, nothing will change this, this is my land. Mine, and only mine. This is the land my forefathers dreamed of. The agreement of the nations to establish this state was made possible by the blood of the six million murdered. I have fought for this country, this strip of land. For the right to be a proud Jew, to raise a free and proud Jewish family. Only here can I defend myself against all those who wish to take my life. Yes, Jerusalem is my home and Israel is my homeland, for Dalia my wife, and my daughter Hila.

I will live and die in Jerusalem, on my land. Only in Israel will I be able to call any place home.

The car stopped and the guest's thoughts were cut off at once. He forced himself to sit up and focus on the girl, taking an active part in her experience.

They were surrounded by a happy clamor as they were taken by a tiny train from the parking lot to the gates of Disneyland.

The closer they got, the more fidgety and restless the girl became, unable to contain her excitement. A colorful world full of magic and charm welcomed them. They smiled, wandering among the costumed characters, surrounded by the smell of popcorn and clouds of cotton candy, humming along with the familiar tunes. The girl ran with a flushed faced between the stores and the different buildings, and soon enough the merriment infected everyone, and they also boarded the various rides, sailed ships and drove tiny cars, swaying in the pleasure of zero gravity.

After long hours of fun the adults' body language showed signs of pleasant fatigue. Irving took the guest's arm, aware of their imminent parting. Together they stood watching the girl – Aaron's granddaughter, soaring above the ground, her dress fluttering like a colorful butterfly, her laughter ringing out above them, and her sparkling eyes peering at the horizon.

Me and my parents, Aaron and Hermina after the war

Me and my uncle Joseph after his return from Transnistria.

Printed in Great Britain
by Amazon